The Naught[...]
in the Sc[...]

Little Elizabeth Allen is rich, pretty and spoilt. She has her own pony and dog and everything she wants at home, and so when her parents send her to boarding-school she is horrified. She doesn't want to make friends with other girls and boys, she doesn't want to share anything with others and she's sure she'll hate every minute of it. So Elizabeth decides to be the naughtiest girl in the school and get sent home again as soon as possible!

Enid Blyton needs no introduction to her readers. Author of around four hundred books, which have been translated into almost every language, she has been known and loved by children of all ages for many years.

Other Enid Blyton titles available in Beaver

The naughtiest girl in the school

Enid Blyton

Illustrated by Gareth Floyd

Beaver Books

A Beaver Book

Published by Arrow Books Limited
62-65 Chandos Place, London WC2N 4NW

A division of Century Hutchinson Ltd

London Melbourne Sydney Auckland
Johannesburg and agencies throughout
the world

First published in 1940 by George Newnes Limited
Beaver edition 1979
Seventh impression 1988

Set in Baskerville

Printed and bound in Great Britain by
Anchor Press Ltd, Tiptree, Essex

ISBN 0 09 945500 5

Contents

1 The naughty spoilt girl

'You'll have to go to school, Elizabeth!' said Mrs Allen. 'I think your governess is quite right. You are spoilt and naughty, and although Daddy and I were going to leave you here with Miss Scott when we went away, I think it would be better for you to go to school.'

Elizabeth stared at her mother in dismay. What, leave her home? And her pony and her dog? Go and be with a lot of children she would hate? Oh no, she wouldn't go!

'I'll be good with Miss Scott,' she said.

'You've said that before,' said her mother. 'Miss Scott says she can't stay with you any longer. Elizabeth, is it true that you put earwigs in her bed last night?'

Elizabeth giggled. 'Yes,' she said. 'Miss Scott is so frightened of them! It's silly to be afraid of earwigs, isn't it?'

'It is much sillier to put them into somebody's bed,' said Mrs Allen sternly. 'You have been spoilt, and you think you can do what you like! You are an only child, and we love you so much, Daddy and I, that I think we have given you too many lovely things, and allowed you too much freedom.'

'Mummy, if you send me to school, I shall be so naughty there that they'll send me back home again,' said Elizabeth, shaking her curls back. She was a pretty girl with laughing blue eyes and dark brown curls. All her life she had done as she liked. Six governesses had come and gone, but not one of them had been able to make Elizabeth obedient or good-mannered!

'You can be such a nice little girl!' they had all said to her, 'but all you think of is getting into mischief and being rude about it!'

And now when she said that she would be so naughty at school that they would have to send her home, her mother looked at her in despair. She loved Elizabeth very much, and wanted her to be happy – but how could she be happy if she did not learn to be as other children were?

'You have been alone too much, Elizabeth,' she said. 'You should have had other children to play with and to work with.'

'I don't like other children!' said Elizabeth sulkily. It was quite true – she didn't like boys and girls at all! They were shocked at her mischief and rude ways, and when they said they wouldn't join in her naughtiness, she laughed at them and said they were babies. Then they told her what they thought of her, and Elizabeth didn't like it.

So now the thought of going away to school and living with other boys and girls made Elizabeth feel dreadful!

'Please don't send me,' she begged. 'I really will be good at home.'

'No, Elizabeth,' said her mother. 'Daddy and I *must* go away for a whole year, and as Miss Scott won't stay, and we could not expect to find another governess quickly before we go, it is best you should go to school. You have a good brain and you should be able to do your work well and get to the top of the form. Then we shall be proud of you.'

'I shan't work at all,' said Elizabeth, pouting. 'I won't work a bit, and they'll think I'm so stupid they won't keep me!'

'Well, Elizabeth, if you want to make things difficult for yourself, you'll have to,' said Mother, getting up. 'We have written to Miss Belle and Miss Best, who run Whyteleafe School, and they are willing to take you next week, when the new term begins. Miss Scott will get all your things ready. Please help her all you can.'

Elizabeth was very angry and upset. She didn't want to go to school. She hated everybody, especially silly children! Miss Scott was horrid to say she wouldn't stay.

Suddenly Elizabeth wondered if she *would* stay, if she asked her very, very nicely!

She ran to find her governess. Miss Scott was busy sewing Elizabeth's name on to a pile of brown stockings.

'Are these new stockings?' asked Elizabeth, in surprise. 'I don't wear stockings! I wear socks!'

'You have to wear stockings at Whyteleafe School,' said Miss Scott. Elizabeth stared at the pile, and then she suddenly put her arms round Miss Scott's neck.

'Miss Scott!' she said. 'Stay with me! I know I'm sometimes naughty, but I don't want you to go.'

'What you *really* mean is that you don't want to go to school,' said Miss Scott. 'I suppose Mother's been telling you?'

'Yes, she has,' said Elizabeth. 'Miss Scott, I *won't* go to school!'

'Well, of course, if you're such a baby as to be afraid of doing what all other children do, then I've nothing more to say,' said Miss Scott, beginning to sew another name on a brown stocking.

Elizabeth stood up at once and stamped her foot. 'Afraid!' she shouted. '*I'm* not afraid! Was I afraid when I fell off my pony? Was I afraid when our car crashed into the bank? Was I afraid when – when – when—'

'Don't shout at me, please, Elizabeth,' said Miss Scott. 'I think you are afraid to go to school and mix with obedient, well-mannered, hard-working children who are not spoilt as you are. You know quite well that you wouldn't get your own way, that you would have to share everything, instead of having things to yourself as you do now, and that you would have to be punctual, polite, and obedient. And you are afraid to go!'

'I'm not, I'm not, I'm not!' shouted Elizabeth. 'I shall go! But I shall be so naughty and lazy that they won't keep me, and then I'll come back home! And you'll have to look after me again, so there!'

'My dear Elizabeth, I shan't be here,' said Miss Scott, taking another stocking. 'I am going to another family, where I shall have two little boys to teach. I am going the day you go to school. So you can't come back home because I shan't be here, your father and mother will be away, and the house will be shut up!'

Elizabeth burst into tears. She sobbed so loudly that Miss Scott, who was really fond of the spoilt, naughty girl, put her arms round her and comforted her.

'Now don't be silly,' she said. 'Most children simply *love* school. It's great fun. You play games, you go for walks, all together, you have the most lovely lessons, and you will make such a lot of friends. You have no friends now, and it is a dreadful thing not to have a single friend. You are very lucky.'

'I'm not,' wept Elizabeth. 'Nobody loves me. I'm very unhappy.'

'The trouble is that people have loved you too much,' said Miss Scott. 'You are pretty, and merry, and rich, so you have been spoilt. People like the way you look, the way you smile, and your pretty clothes so they fuss you, and pet you, and spoil you, instead of treating you like an ordinary child. But it isn't enough to have a pretty face and a merry smile – you must have a good heart too.'

Nobody had spoken to Elizabeth like this before, and the little girl was astonished. 'I *have* got a good heart,' she said, tossing her curls back again.

'Well, you don't show it much!' said Miss Scott. 'Now run away, please, because I've got to count all these stockings, and then mark your new vests and bodices.'

Elizabeth looked at the pile of stockings. She hated them. Nasty brown things! She wouldn't wear them! She'd take her socks to school and wear *those* if she wanted to! Miss Scott turned to a chest-of-drawers and began to take out some vests. Elizabeth picked up two brown stockings and pinned them toe to toe. Then she tiptoed to Miss Scott and neatly and quietly pinned them to her skirt.

She skipped out of the room, giggling. Miss Scott car-

ried the vests to the table. She began to count the stockings. There should be six pairs.

'One – two – three – four – five,' she counted. 'Five.
Dear me – where's the sixth?'

She looked on the floor. She looked on the chair. She
was really vexed. She counted the pile again. Then she
went to the door and looked for Elizabeth. The little girl
was pulling something out of a cupboard on the landing.

'Elizabeth!' called Miss Scott sharply, 'have you got a
pair of brown stockings?'

'No, Miss Scott,' said Elizabeth, making her eyes look
round and surprised. 'Why?'

'Because a pair is missing,' said Miss Scott. 'Did you
take them out of this room?'

'No, really, Miss Scott,' said Elizabeth truthfully, trying not to laugh as she caught sight of the stockings swinging at Miss Scott's back. 'I'm sure all the stockings are in the room, Miss Scott, really!'

'Then perhaps your mother has a pair,' said Miss Scott. 'I'll go and ask her.'

Off marched the governess down the landing, the pinned brown stockings trailing behind her like a tail. Elizabeth put her head into the cupboard and squealed with laughter. Miss Scott went into her mother's room.

'Excuse me, Mrs Allen,' she said, 'but have you one of Elizabeth's new pairs of stockings? I've only five pairs.'

'No, I gave you them all,' said Mrs Allen, surprised. 'They must be together. Perhaps you have dropped them somewhere.'

Miss Scott turned to go, and Mrs Allen caught sight of the brown stockings following Miss Scott. She looked at them in astonishment.

'Wait, Miss Scott,' she said. 'What's this!' She went to Miss Scott, and unpinned the stockings. The governess looked at Mrs Allen.

'Elizabeth, of course!' she said.

'Yes, Elizabeth!' said Mrs Allen. 'Always in mischief. I really never knew such a child in my life. It is high time she went to school. Don't you agree, Miss Scott?'

'I do,' said Miss Scott heartily. 'You will see a different and much nicer child when you come back home again, Mrs Allen!'

Elizabeth was passing by, and heard what her mother and her governess were saying. She hit the door with the book she was carrying and shouted angrily.

'You won't see me any different, Mother, you won't, you won't! I'll be worse!'

'You couldn't be!' said Mrs Allen in despair. 'You really *couldn't* be worse!'

2   Elizabeth goes to school

For the rest of her time at home Elizabeth was very naughty and also very good.

'I'll try being very, very good and obedient and polite and sweet, and see if Mother changes her mind,' she thought. So, to the surprise of everyone, she became thoughtful, sweet-tongued, good-mannered, and most obedient. But it had quite the wrong effect, because, instead of saying that she would keep her at home now, her mother said something quite different!

'Well, Elizabeth, now that I know what a really nice girl you can be, I'm not so afraid of sending you to school as I was,' she said. 'I thought you would get into such trouble and be so unhappy – but now that I see how well you really can behave, I am sure you will get on nicely at school. I am very pleased with your behaviour!'

And you can guess what happened after that. Elizabeth at once became naughtier than she had ever been before!

'If being good makes Mother feel like that, I'll see what being naughty does!' she thought.

So she emptied the ink-bottle over the cushions in the drawing-room. She tore a hole in one of the nicest curtains. She put three black beetles into poor Miss Scott's toothbrush mug, and she squeezed the seccotine into the ends of both Miss Scott's brown shoes, so that her toes would stick there!

'Well, all this makes it quite certain that Elizabeth needs to go to school!' said Miss Scott angrily, as she tried to get her feet out of her sticky shoes. 'I'm glad to leave her! Naughty little girl! And yet she can be so sweet and nice when she likes.'

Elizabeth's things were packed and ready. She had a neat brown trunk, with 'E. Allen' painted on it in black. She had a tuck-box too, with a big currant cake inside, a box of chocolate, a tin of toffee, a jam sandwich, and a tin of shortbread.

'You will have to share these things with the others,' said Miss Scott, as she packed the things neatly inside.

'Well, I shan't, then,' said Elizabeth.

'Very well, don't!' said Miss Scott. 'If you want to show everyone what a selfish child you are, just take the chance!'

Elizabeth put on the outdoor uniform of Whyteleafe School. It was very neat, and she looked nice in it. But then Elizabeth looked nice in anything!

The outdoor uniform was a dark blue coat with a yellow edge to the collar and cuffs, a dark blue hat with a yellow ribbon round it, and the school badge at the front. Her stockings were long and brown, and her lace shoes were brown too.

'My goodness, you do look a real schoolgirl!' said her mother, quite proudly. Elizabeth wouldn't smile. She stood there, sulky and angry. 'I shan't stay at school long,' she said. 'They'll soon send me back!'

'Don't be silly, Elizabeth,' said her mother. She kissed the little girl goodbye and hugged her. 'I will come and see you at half-term,' she said.

'No, Mother, you won't,' said Elizabeth. 'I shall be home long before that!'

'Don't make me sad, Elizabeth!' said Mrs Allen. But Elizabeth wouldn't smile or say she was sorry. She got into the car that was to take her to the station, and sat there, very cross and straight. She had said goodbye to her pony. She had said goodbye to Timmy, her dog. She had said goodbye to her canary. And to each of them she had whispered the same thing.

'I'll soon be back! You'll see – they won't keep the naughtiest girl in the school for long!'

Miss Scott took her to the station and then up to London in the train. She went with Elizabeth to a big station where trains whistled and chuffed, and people ran about in a hurry.

'Now we must find the right platform,' said Miss Scott, hurrying too. 'We have to meet the teacher there, who is in charge of the girls going by this train.'

They came to the right platform and went through to

where a big group of girls stood with a teacher. They were all dressed in dark blue coats and hats, with yellow hatbands like Elizabeth. The girls were of all ages, some big, some small, and most of them were chattering hard.

Two or three stood apart, looking shy. They were the new ones, like Elizabeth. The teacher spoke to them now and again, and they smiled gratefully at her.

Miss Scott bustled up to the teacher. 'Good morning,' she said. 'Is this Miss Thomas? This is Elizabeth Allen. I'm glad we are in good time!'

'Good morning,' said Miss Thomas, smiling. She held out her hand to Elizabeth. 'Well, dear,' she said, 'so you are going to join the happy crowd at Whyteleafe School!'

Elizabeth put her hand behind her back and would not shake hands with Miss Thomas. The teacher looked surprised. The other children stared. Miss Scott blushed red, and spoke sharply to Elizabeth.

'Elizabeth! Shake hands at once!'

Elizabeth turned her back and looked at a train puffing nearby. 'I'm so sorry she's behaving so rudely,' said Miss Scott, really upset. She spoke in a low voice to Miss Thomas. 'She's an only child – very, very spoilt – rich, pretty – and she doesn't want to come away to school. Just leave her alone for a bit and I expect she'll be all right.'

Miss Thomas nodded. She was a merry-looking young woman, and the girls liked her. She was just going to say something when a man came hurrying up with four boys.

'Good morning, Miss Thomas,' he said. 'Here is my batch! Sorry I can't stop, I've a train to catch! Goodbye, boys!'

'Goodbye, sir,' said the four boys.

'How many boys have you at Whyteleafe this term?' asked Miss Scott. 'As many as girls?'

'Not quite,' said Miss Thomas. 'There are some more boys over there, look, in charge of Mr Johns.'

Miss Scott liked the look of the boys, all in dark blue overcoats and blue caps with yellow badges in front. 'Such a good idea,' she said, 'to educate boys and girls together.

For a child like Elizabeth, who has no brothers, and not even a sister, it is like joining a large family of brothers and sisters and cousins, to go to a school like Whyteleafe !'

'Oh, they'll soon knock the corners off your Elizabeth,' smiled Miss Thomas. 'Look – here comes our train. We have our carriages reserved for us, so I must find them. The boys have two carriages and the girls have three. Come along, girls, here's our train !'

Elizabeth was swept along with the others. She was pushed into a carriage with a big label on it, 'Reserved for Whyteleafe School.'

'Goodbye, Elizabeth; goodbye, dear !' cried Miss Scott. 'Do your best !'

'Goodbye,' said Elizabeth, suddenly feeling very small and lost. 'I'll soon be back !' she shouted.

'Gracious !' said a tubby little girl next to her, 'a term's a long time, you know ! Fancy saying you'll soon be back !'

'Well, I shall,' said Elizabeth. She was squashed in a heap by the tubby little girl and another girl on the other side, who was rather bony. She didn't like it.

Elizabeth felt sure she would never, never learn who all the different girls were. She felt a little afraid of the big ones, and she was horrified to think there were boys at her school ! Boys ! Nasty, rough creatures – well, she'd show them that a girl could be rough too !

The little girl sat silently as the train rattled on and on. The others chattered and talked and offered sweets round the carriage. Elizabeth shook her head when the sweets were offered to her.

'Oh, come on, do have one !' said the tubby little girl, whose sweets they were. 'A sweet would do you good – make you look a bit sweeter perhaps !'

Everybody laughed. Elizabeth went red and hated the tubby little girl.

'Ruth ! You do say some funny things !' said a big girl opposite. 'Don't tease the poor little thing. She's new.'

'Well, so is Belinda, next to you,' said Ruth, 'but she does at least *say* something when she's spoken to !'

'That will do, Ruth,' said Miss Thomas, seeing how red Elizabeth had gone. Ruth said no more, but the next time she offered her sweets round she did not offer them to Elizabeth.

It was a long journey. Elizabeth was tired when at last the train drew up in a country station and the girls poured out of the carriages. The boys came to join them, and the children talked eagerly of all they had done in the holidays.

'Come along now, quickly,' said Mr Johns, pushing them out of the station gate. 'The coach is waiting.'

There was an enormous coach outside the station, labelled 'Whyteleafe School'. The children took their places. Elizabeth found a place as far away as possible from the tubby little girl called Ruth. She didn't like her one bit. She didn't like Belinda either. She didn't like anyone! They all stared at her too much!

The coach set off with a loud clank and rumble. Round the corner it went, down a country lane, up a steep hill – and there was Whyteleafe School at the top! It was a beautiful building, like an old country house – which, indeed, it once had been. Its deep red walls, green with creeper, glowed in the April sun. It had a broad flight of steps leading from the green lawns up to the school terrace.

'Good old Whyteleafe!' said Ruth, pleased to see it. The coach swept round to the other side of the school, through a great archway, and up to the front door. The children jumped down and ran up the steps, shouting and laughing.

Elizabeth found her hand taken by Miss Thomas. 'Welcome to Whyteleafe, Elizabeth!' said the teacher kindly, smiling down at the sulky face. 'I am sure you will do well here and be very happy with us all.'

'I shan't,' said naughty Elizabeth, and she pulled her hand away! It was certainly not a very good beginning.

3 Elizabeth makes a bad beginning

It was half-past one by the time the children arrived, and they were all hungry for their dinner. They were told to wash their hands quickly, and tidy themselves and then go to the dining-hall for their dinner.

'Eileen, please look after the three new girls,' said Miss Thomas. A big girl, with a kindly face and a mass of fair curls, came up to Belinda, Elizabeth, and another girl called Helen. She gave them a push in the direction of the cloakrooms.

'Hurry!' she said. So they hurried, and Elizabeth soon found herself in a big cloakroom, tiled in gleaming white, with basins down one side, and mirrors here and there.

She washed quickly, feeling rather lost in such a crowd of chattering girls. Helen and Belinda had made friends, and Elizabeth wished they would say something to her instead of chattering to one another. But they said nothing to Elizabeth, thinking her rude and queer.

Then to the dining-hall went all the girls and took their places. The boys clattered in too.

'Sit anywhere you like today,' said a tall mistress, whose name, Elizabeth found, was Miss Belle. So the children sat down and began to eat their dinner hungrily. There was hot soup first, then beef, carrots, dumplings, onions and potatoes, and then rice pudding and golden syrup. Elizabeth was so hungry that she ate everything put before her, though at home she would certainly have pushed away the rice pudding.

As it was the first day the children were allowed to talk as they pleased, and there was such a noise as they told one another what they had done in the holidays.

'I had a puppy for Easter,' said one girl with a laughing face. 'Do you know, my father bought a simply enormous

Easter egg, and put the puppy inside, and tied up the egg with a red ribbon? Goodness, didn't I laugh when I undid it!'

Everybody else laughed too.

'I had a new bicycle for *my* Easter present,' said a round-faced boy. 'But it wasn't put into an egg!'

'What did *you* have for Easter?' said Eileen to Elizabeth in a kindly tone. She was sitting opposite, and felt sorry for the silent new girl. Belinda and Helen were sitting together, telling each other about the last school they had been to. Only Elizabeth had no one to talk to her.

'I had a guinea-pig,' said Elizabeth, in a clear voice, 'and it had a face just like Miss Thomas.'

There was a shocked silence. Somebody giggled. Miss Thomas looked rather surprised, but she said nothing.

'If you weren't a new girl, you'd be jolly well sat on for that!' said a girl nearby, glaring at Elizabeth. 'Rude creature!'

Elizabeth couldn't help going red. She had made up her mind to be naughty and rude, and she was going to be really bad, but it was rather dreadful to have somebody speaking like that to her, in front of everyone. She went on with her rice pudding. Soon the children began to talk to one another again, and Elizabeth was forgotten.

After dinner the boys went to unpack their things in their own bedrooms, and the girls went to theirs.

'Whose room are the new girls in, please, Miss Thomas?' asked Eileen. Miss Thomas looked at her list.

'Let me see,' she said, 'yes – here we are – Elizabeth Allen, Belinda Green, Helen Marsden – they are all in Room Six, Eileen, and with them are Ruth James, Joan Lesley and Nora O'Sullivan. Ask Nora to take the new girls there and show them what to do. She's head of that room.'

'Nora! Hi, Nora!' called Eileen, as a tall, dark-haired girl, with deep blue eyes went by. 'Take these kids to Room Six, will you? They're yours! You're head of that room.'

'I know,' said Nora, looking at the three new girls. 'Hallo, is this the girl who was rude to Miss Thomas? You just mind what you say, whatever-your-name-is, I'm not having any cheek from *you*!'

'I shall say exactly what I like,' said Elizabeth boldly. '*You* can't stop me!'

'Oho, can't I?' said Nora, her blue Irish eyes glaring at Elizabeth. 'That's all *you* know! Get along to the bedroom now, and I'll show you all what to do.'

They all went up a winding oak staircase and came to a wide landing. All around it were doors, marked with numbers. Nora opened the door of Number Six and went in.

The bedroom was long, high and airy. There were wide windows, all open to the school gardens outside. The sun poured in and made the room look very pleasant indeed.

The room was divided into six by blue curtains, which were now drawn back to the walls, so that six low white beds could be seen, each with a blue eiderdown. Beside each bed stood a wide chest-of-drawers, with a small mirror on top. The chests were painted white with blue wooden handles, and looked very pretty.

There were three wash-basins in the room, with hot and cold water taps, to be shared by the six girls. There was also a tall white cupboard for each girl, and in these they hung their coats and dresses.

Each bed had a blue rug beside it on the polished brown boards. Elizabeth couldn't help thinking that it all looked rather exciting. She had only slept with Miss Scott before – now she was to sleep with five other girls!

'Your trunks and tuck-boxes are beside your beds,' said Nora. 'You must each unpack now, and put your things away tidily. And when I say tidily I *mean* tidily. I shall look at your drawers once a week. On the top of the chest you are allowed to have six things, not more. Choose what you like – hairbrushes, or photographs, or ornaments – it doesn't matter.'

'How silly!' thought Elizabeth scornfully, thinking of

her own untidy dressing-table at home. 'I shall put as many things out as I like!'

They all began unpacking. Elizabeth had never packed or unpacked anything in her life, and she found it rather exciting. She put her things neatly away in her chest-of-drawers – the piles of stockings, vests, bodices, blouses, everything she had brought with her. She hung up her school coat and her dresses.

The others were busy unpacking too. Whilst they were doing this two more girls danced into the room.

'Hallo, Nora!' said one, a red-haired girl with freckles all over her face. I'm in your room this term. Good!'

'Hallo, Joan,' said Nora. 'Get on with your unpacking, there's a lamb. Hallo, Ruth – I've got you here again, have I? Well, just see you're a bit tidier than last term!'

Ruth laughed. She was the girl who had handed round her sweets in the train, and she was plump and clever. She ran to her trunk and began to undo it.

Nora began to tell the new girls a little about the school. They listened as they busily put away their things in their drawers.

'Whyteleafe School isn't a very large school,' began Nora, 'but it's a jolly fine one. The boys have their lessons with us, and we play tennis and cricket with them and we have our own teams of girls only, too. Last year we beat the boys at tennis. We'll beat them this year, too, if only we can get some good players. Any of you new girls play tennis?'

Belinda did but the others didn't. Nora went on talking, as she hung up her dresses.

'We all have the same amount of pocket-money to spend,' she said. 'And it's plenty too. Two shillings a week.'

'I shall have a lot more than that,' said Belinda in surprise.

'Oh no, you won't,' said Nora. 'All the money we have is put into a big box, and we each draw two shillings a week from it, unless we've been fined for something.'

'What do you mean – fined?' asked Helen. 'Who fines us? Miss Belle and Miss Best?'

'Oh no,' said Nora. 'We hold a big meeting once a week – oftener, if necessary – and we hear complaints and grumbles, and if anyone has been behaving badly we fine them. Miss Belle or Miss Best come to the meeting too, of course, but they don't decide anything much. They trust us to decide for ourselves.'

Elizabeth thought this was very strange. She had always thought that the teachers punished the children – but at Whyteleafe it seemed as if the children did it! She listened in astonishment to all that Nora was saying.

'If there's any money over, it is given to anyone who particularly wants to buy something that the meeting approves of,' went on Nora. 'For instance, suppose you broke your tennis racket, Belinda, and needed a new one, the meeting might allow you to take the money from the box to buy one – especially if they thought you were a very good player.'

'I see,' said Belinda. 'It sounds a good idea. Look, Nora – here are the things out of my tuck-box. What do I do with them? I want to share them with everybody.'

'Thanks,' said Nora. 'Well, we keep all our cakes and sweets and things in the playroom downstairs. There's a big cupboard there, and tins to put cakes into. I'll show you where. Elizabeth, are your tuck-box things ready? If so, bring them along, and we'll put them into the cupboard to share at tea-time.'

'I'm not going to share,' said Elizabeth, remembering that she hadn't been naughty or horrid for some time. 'I shall eat them all myself.'

There was a horrified silence. The five girls stared at Elizabeth as if they couldn't believe their ears. Not share her cakes and sweets? Whatever sort of a girl was this?

'Well,' said Nora, at last, her merry face suddenly very disgusted. 'You can do what you like, of course, with your own things. If they're as horrid as you seem to be, nobody would want to eat them!'

4   Elizabeth gets into trouble

As Nora was about to lead the way down to the playroom, she glanced at the chests-of-drawers to see that they were tidy on the top. To her surprise she saw that Elizabeth had put about a dozen things on her chest!

Nora stopped and looked at them. There were two hairbrushes, a mirror, a comb, three photographs, a bottle of scent, two small vases, and a clothes-brush.

'Look here!' said Nora, to the others, 'this poor child can't count up to six! She's got eleven things on her chest. Poor Elizabeth! Fancy not being able to count six.'

'I *can*,' said Elizabeth fiercely. 'One, two, three, four, five, six.'

Everybody squealed with laughter. 'She *can* count!' said Nora. 'Well, Elizabeth, count your things, and take five away – or can't you do taking-away? There are eleven things on your chest – take away five – and it will leave six – which is the number I told you to have.'

'I'm not going to take any away,' said Elizabeth rudely.

'Aren't you?' said Nora, in surprise. 'Well, if you won't – I will!'

The angry Irish girl picked up a hairbrush, the three photographs, and the mirror. She went to a box under the window, took a key from her pocket and unlocked it. She put the five things inside and locked the box.

'That's what happens when people can't count,' she said. Elizabeth stared at her in a rage.

'Give me my things back,' she said. 'I want those photographs at once! They are of Mummy and Daddy and my pony too.'

'Sorry,' said Nora, putting the key into her pocket. 'You

can have them back when you apologize, and tell me that you know how to count.'

'I shan't,' said Elizabeth.

'Just as you please,' said Nora. 'Now come on, everybody, and let's take the eatables down to the playroom.'

'I don't want to bring mine,' said Elizabeth. 'I want to leave them here.'

'Well, if you do, they'll go into that box along with the photographs,' said Nora firmly. 'The rule is that all eatables go downstairs.'

Elizabeth stood sulking, looking at her cake, her jam sandwich, her chocolate, toffee, and shortbread. Then she picked up her tuck-box and followed the others. She did not want them to go into that box! She had seen enough of Nora to know that that young lady was very determined!

They clattered down the oak staircase. At one side of the hall was an open door, leading into a very large room lined with cupboards and bookcases. It was full of boys and girls.

Some were talking, some were playing games, some were putting away cakes into tins. They were all busy and happy, and called out greetings to Nora as she came into the room.

There was a gramophone going in one corner. Elizabeth stopped to listen to it, for she loved music. It was playing a tune that her mother played at home, and suddenly the little girl felt as if she wanted her mother badly.

'But, never mind!' she thought to herself. 'I shan't be here long! I don't expect they'll keep me more than a week if I go on being awfully naughty.'

'Here are some empty tins,' said Nora, handing some down from a shelf. 'Catch, Helen. Catch, Elizabeth. Here's a big one for you, Belinda, to take in that enormous cake!'

Soon they were all putting away their things. Nora took slips of paper from a pile and wrote their names on. 'Stick your name on your tin,' she said, licking hers and sticking it to the side of her tin.

'I'd like to see the classrooms,' said Belinda. Ruth said she would show her round the whole school, and off she went with Belinda and Helen. Elizabeth followed a little way behind, curious to see what a school was like, for she had never seen inside one before.

The dining-hall she had already seen – a great high room, with big windows. Tables ran down the middle of it. It was only used for meals.

Then there were the classrooms, big, sunny rooms all over the place, with neat desks and chairs, and a bigger desk for the teacher. There were blackboards everywhere, just like the one that Miss Scott had used for Elizabeth.

'This is *our* classroom,' said Ruth to the new girls. 'I expect we'll all be in Miss Ranger's class. She's pretty strict, I can tell you! Nora's in a higher class, of course. She's older. She's a jolly good sort, don't you think so?'

'Yes,' agreed Helen and Belinda at once. But Elizabeth thought differently. She pursed up her mouth and said nothing.

'This is the gym,' said Ruth, and the three new girls looked in wonder at the great room, with its ropes and climbing-ladders, and bars and poles. Elizabeth suddenly felt excited. She loved climbing and swinging and jumping. She hoped she could do some gym before she left.

There were many other bedrooms like her own, and then there was the part of the house put aside for Miss Belle and Miss Best and the other teachers.

'You'll each have to go and see the heads after tea,' said Ruth. 'They're good sorts.'

By the time the four girls had gone over the lovely grounds and had seen the cricket-fields, the tennis-courts, and the flower-filled gardens, it was time for tea. A bell rang loudly, and the girls looked cheerful.

'Good! Tea!' said Ruth. 'Come on. Wash first, all of you, and do your hairs. Yours looks awful, Elizabeth.'

Elizabeth did not like her dark curls being called 'awful'. She went up to her bedroom and did her hair neatly, and washed her hands. She was very hungry, and thought with pleasure of her currant cake and jam sandwich.

'I've got the most gorgeous chocolate cake you ever saw!' said Belinda to the others. 'It just melts in your mouth! You must all have a piece.'

'And I've got some home-made shrimp-paste that's too delicious for words,' said Ruth. 'You wait till you taste it.'

Chocolate cake and home-made shrimp-paste seemed even more delicious to Elizabeth than currant cake and jam sandwich, which suddenly seemed rather ordinary. She ran downstairs wondering if she would have *two* pieces of Belinda's gorgeous chocolate cake.

Tea was laid in the dining-room. The long tables were spread with white cloths, and plates with big slices of brown bread and butter were set all the way down. There were some large plain cakes here and there, and some big pots of plum jam.

The children put their tuck-boxes on a bare table, and placed on some empty plates there the cake or sandwich, jam or paste they meant to share at tea. These plates they took to their own table.

Once again they were allowed to sit where they liked. Elizabeth put out her sandwich and her currant cake and took her place too. Grace was said and then the boys and girls began to chatter quietly.

Suddenly Nora banged on the table. She was at the head of it. Everyone at her table stopped speaking.

'I nearly forgot to say something,' said Nora. 'Elizabeth Allen does not wish to share her things with anyone, so don't ask her for a piece of her cake, will you? She wants it all herself.'

'All right!' said the other children, and they stared at Elizabeth in surprise. Elizabeth went on eating her bread and butter. Next to her was Ruth, opening a large pot of shrimp-paste that smelt simply delicious. She passed it round the table – but did not offer Elizabeth any.

Nobody offered her anything at all. Belinda counted how many there were at the table – eleven – and then cut her cake into *ten* big pieces. Ten was enough, because she missed Elizabeth out! Elizabeth watched the others munching the chocolate cake, which looked and smelt marvellous and longed for a piece.

She cut her currant cake. It looked quite nice. She suddenly felt that she really couldn't eat it all by herself, she *must* offer it to the others too. She didn't mind being thought naughty, but being thought mean was different.

'Will you have a piece of my cake?' she asked Ruth.

Ruth stared at her in surprise. 'How you do change your mind!' she said. 'No thanks. I've had enough.'

Elizabeth offered her cake to Belinda. Belinda shook her head. 'No, thank you,' she said. Elizabeth held out her plate to Helen, but Helen simply made a face at her and turned away.

Nobody would have any of Elizabeth's cake or of her sandwich either. Everyone else had either cut up half or all their cakes, and had finished up their pots of jam or paste. Only Elizabeth's cake and sandwich stood almost untouched on their plates.

A bell rang. Miss Thomas stood up and spoke to the girls and boys. 'You may go out to play,' she said, 'but the new children must stay behind in the playroom, and see the headmistresses.'

So Helen, Elizabeth, and Belinda went to the playroom, and also two boys named Kenneth and Ronald. They set the gramophone going. Belinda did a funny dance and made them all laugh.

Then someone poked her head in at the door and called to the children.

'Miss Belle and Miss Best are waiting to see you. Go and line up outside the drawing-room door – and mind you each say you're going to do your best for Whyteleafe School, and will work and play hard!'

The girl disappeared. The new children went to line up outside the drawing-room door. It opened and Miss Best appeared. 'Come in,' she said to Belinda, and in Belinda went. The door shut.

'Well, *I'm* not going to say I shall work hard and play hard,' said Elizabeth to herself. 'I'm going just to warn them that I won't stay here and I'll be so bad they'll have to send me away. I *won't* stay at this horrid school!'

The door opened and Belinda came out, smiling. 'You're to go in next, Elizabeth,' she said. 'And for goodness' sake behave yourself!'

5 Elizabeth is naughty

Elizabeth pushed open the door and went into the big drawing-room. It was a lovely room, with a few beautiful pictures on the walls, and glowing cushions on the chairs and the couches. The two mistresses were sitting on chairs near the window. They looked up as Elizabeth came in.

'Well, Elizabeth! We are very glad to see you at Whyteleafe School,' said Miss Belle. She was young and pretty, but Miss Best was older, and, except when she smiled, she had rather a stern face.

'Sit down, Elizabeth,' said Miss Best, smiling her lovely smile. 'I hope you have made a few friends already.'

'No, I haven't,' said Elizabeth. She sat down on a chair. Miss Best looked at her in surprise, when she answered so shortly.

'Well, I expect you will soon make plenty,' said the headmistress. 'I hope you will be very happy with us, Elizabeth.'

'I shan't be,' said Elizabeth in a rude voice.

'What a funny little girl!' said Miss Belle, and she laughed. 'Cheer up, dear – you'll soon find things are very jolly here, and I am sure you will do your best to work hard, and make us proud of you.'

'I'm not going to,' said Elizabeth, going red. 'I'm going to be as bad and naughty and horrid as I can possibly be, so there! I don't want to go to school. I hate Whyteleafe School! I'll be so bad that you'll send me home next week!'

The little girl glared at the two mistresses as she said all this, expecting them to jump up in anger. Instead they both threw back their heads and laughed and laughed!

'Oh, Elizabeth, what an extraordinary child you are!' said Miss Belle, wiping away the tears of laughter that had come into her eyes. 'You look such a good, pretty little girl too – no one would think you wanted to be so bad and naughty and horrid!'

'I don't care how you punish me,' said Elizabeth, tears coming into her own eyes – but tears of anger, not of laughter. 'You can do all you like – I just shan't care!'

'We never punish anyone, Elizabeth,' said Miss Best, suddenly looking stern again. 'Didn't you know that?'

'No, I didn't,' said Elizabeth in astonishment. 'What do you do when people are naughty, then?'

'Oh, we leave any naughty person to the rest of the children to deal with,' said Miss Best. 'Every week the school holds a meeting, you know, and the children themselves decide what is to be done with boys and girls who don't behave themselves. It won't bother *us* if you are naughty – but you may perhaps find that you make the children angry.'

'That seems funny to me,' said Elizabeth. 'I thought it was always the teachers that did the punishing.'

'Not at Whyteleafe School,' said Miss Belle. 'Well, Elizabeth, my dear, perhaps you'd go now and tell the next child to come in, will you? Maybe one day White-leafe School will be proud of you, even though you are quite sure it won't!'

Elizabeth went out without another word. She couldn't help liking the two headmistresses, though she didn't want to at all. She wished she had been ruder to them. What a funny school this was!

She spoke to Helen outside the door. 'You're to go in now,' she said. 'The Beauty and the Beast are waiting for you!'

'Oh, you naughty girl!' said Helen, with a giggle. 'Miss Belle and Miss Best – the Beauty and the Beast! That's rather clever of you to think of that, Elizabeth!'

Elizabeth had meant it to be very rude. She did not know enough of other children to know that they always loved nicknames for their masters and mistresses. She was surprised that Helen thought her clever – and secretly she was pleased.

But she stuck her nose in the air and marched off. *She* wasn't going to be pleased with anything or anybody at Whyteleafe School!

She wandered round by herself until the supper-bell went at seven o'clock. She felt hungry and went into the dining-hall. The children were once more opening their tins of cakes, and a lively chatter was going on. It all looked very jolly.

There were big mugs on the table and big jugs of steaming hot cocoa here and there. There were piles of bread again, butter, cheese, and dishes of stewed fruit. The children sat down and helped themselves.

Nobody took any notice of Elizabeth at all, till suddenly Helen remembered what she had called Miss Belle and Miss Best. With a giggle she repeated it to her neighbour, and soon there was laughter all round the table.

'The Beauty and the Beast,' went the whisper, and chuckles echoed round. Elizabeth heard the whispers and went red. Nora O'Sullivan laughed loudly.

'It's a jolly good nickname!' she said. 'Belle means Beauty, and Best is very like Beast – and certainly Miss Belle is lovely, and Miss Best isn't! That was pretty smart of you, Elizabeth.'

Elizabeth smiled! She really couldn't help it. She didn't want to – she wanted to be as horrid as possible – but it was really very pleasant to have everyone laughing at her joke.

'It's queer, though,' she thought. 'I meant to be horrid and rude, and the others just think it's funny. I guess Miss Belle and Miss Best wouldn't think it was funny, though!'

Nobody offered Elizabeth any of their goodies, and she did not like to offer hers, for she felt sure everyone would say no. The meal went on until half-past seven, and then after grace was said the children all got up and went to the playroom.

'When's your bedtime?' said Nora to Elizabeth. 'I expect it's eight o'clock. You'd better see. The times are on the notice-board over there. My bedtime is at half-past eight, and when I come to bed I expect all the rest of you to be safe in bed.'

'I don't want to go to bed at eight o'clock,' said Elizabeth indignantly. 'I go to bed much later than that at home.'

'Well, you shouldn't, then,' said Nora. 'No wonder you're such a crosspatch! My mother says that late hours make children stupid, bad-tempered, and slow.'

Elizabeth went to see the times for going to bed. Hers was, as Nora had said, at eight o'clock. Well, she wouldn't go! She'd be naughty!

So she slipped out into the garden and went to where she had seen two or three big swings. She got on to a swing and began to push herself to and fro. It was lovely there in the evening sunshine. Elizabeth quite forgot that she was at school, and she sang a little song to herself.

A boy came into the place where the swings were, and stared at Elizabeth. 'What are you doing here?' he said. 'I bet it's your bedtime!'

'Mind your own business!' said Elizabeth at once.

'Well, what about you going off to bed, and minding *yours*!' said the boy. 'I'm a monitor, and it's my job to see that people do what they're told!'

'I don't know what a monitor is, and I don't care,' said Elizabeth rudely.

'Well, let *me* tell you what a monitor is,' said the boy, who was just about Elizabeth's size. 'It's somebody put in charge of other silly kids at Whyteleafe, to see they don't get *too* silly! If you don't behave yourself I shall have to report you at the Meeting! Then you'll be punished.'

'Pooh!' said Elizabeth, and she swung herself very hard indeed, put out her foot and kicked the boy so vigorously that he fell right over. Elizabeth squealed with laughter – but not for long! The boy jumped up, ran to the swing and shook Elizabeth off. He caught hold of her dark curls

and pulled them so hard that the little girl yelled with pain.

The boy grinned at her and said, 'Serve you right ! You be careful how you treat me next time, or I'll pull your nose as well as your hair ! Now – are you going in or not?'

Elizabeth ran away from him and went indoors. She looked at the clock – quarter-past eight! Perhaps she would have time to go to bed before that horrid Nora came up at half-past.

So she ran up the stairs and went to Bedroom Number 6. Ruth, Joan, Belinda, and Helen were already there half undressed. Their curtains were pulled around their cubicles, but they were talking hard all the same. Elizabeth slipped into her own cubicle.

'You're late, Elizabeth,' said Ruth. 'You'll get into trouble if you're caught by a monitor.'

'I have been,' said Elizabeth. 'But *I* didn't care ! I was on the swing and I put out my foot and kicked him over !'

'Well, you're very silly,' said Ruth. 'You will get into trouble at the Meeting if you don't look out. And that's not pleasant.'

'I don't care for any silly Meeting,' said Elizabeth, jumping into bed. She remembered that Nora had put her three photographs into the locked box, and she jumped out again. She went to the box and tried to open it – but it was still locked. Nora came in at that moment and saw Elizabeth there.

'Hallo, kid,' she said. 'Do you want your things back? Well, apologize and you can have them.'

But Elizabeth was not going to say she was sorry. She made a rude face at Nora, and flung herself into bed.

'Well, you *are* a sweet child, aren't you !' said Nora mockingly. 'I hope you get out at the right side of your bed tomorrow !'

Then there was a creak as Nora sat on her bed to take off her stockings. A clock struck half-past eight downstairs. 'No more talking now,' said Nora. 'Sleep tight, all of you !'

6   Elizabeth joins her class

Elizabeth wondered where she was when she awoke the next morning, but she soon remembered. She was at that horrid school!

A bell rang. Nora sat up in her bed and spoke to the others. 'That's the bell for getting up,' she said. 'Stir your-selves! You've got half an hour.'

Elizabeth thought she wouldn't get up. She lay there warm in her bed, and looked up at the white ceiling. Nora's voice came sharply to her.

'Elizabeth Allen! Are you getting up or are you not?'

'Not,' said Elizabeth cheekily.

'Well, I'm in charge of you five, and it's my job to get you down to breakfast in good time,' said Nora, poking her nose round the curtain. 'Get up, you lazy creature!'

'Are you a monitor?' asked Elizabeth, remembering the boy of the evening before.

'I am,' said Nora. 'Come on, get up, Elizabeth, and don't make yourself such a nuisance.'

Elizabeth still lay there. Nora nodded to plump Ruth, and the two went beside Elizabeth's bed. Together they stripped all the clothes off the lazy girl, and then tipped up the mattress. Elizabeth gave a shriek and slid on to the floor. She was very angry.

She rushed at Nora – but Nora was big and strong, and caught hold of the angry girl's arms at once. 'Don't be silly now,' she said. 'Get dressed and hurry up or I'll spank you with a hairbrush! Monitors do that sometimes, you know!'

Elizabeth felt that she couldn't bear to be spanked by Nora. She washed very sulkily, dressed, cleaned her teeth

37

and did her hair. She was just going downstairs when Nora, who had gone into everyone's cubicle to see if they were tidy, called her back.

'Elizabeth! Come and put your chest-of-drawers tidy! Do you want me to put the rest of your things into the locked box?'

Elizabeth went back and tidied her things. It was quicker to do that than argue with Nora. She wondered if Nora would notice that she had put socks on instead of the long brown stockings!

But Nora didn't notice. She was in too big a hurry to get down to breakfast in time, and besides, she didn't dream that anyone would wear socks instead of stockings at Whyteleafe School!

But a great many of the other children noticed Elizabeth's bare legs at once, and giggled. Miss Thomas noticed them too, and called to Elizabeth.

'You've put the wrong things on, Elizabeth. You must change your socks for stockings afterwards.'

But Elizabeth didn't! When she went up to make her bed afterwards, she didn't change at all. Nora saw that she hadn't and spoke to her.

'For goodness' sake put stockings on, Elizabeth. Really, I shouldn't have thought anyone could be quite so silly as you seem to be!'

'I'm not silly,' said Elizabeth. 'I prefer socks. Stockings make my legs too hot. And I'm going to keep my socks *on*.'

Ruth spoke to Nora. 'Nora, Elizabeth is really babyish,' she said. 'And the babies at Whyteleafe are allowed to wear socks, aren't they? I've seen them in the Kindergarten, with their dear little bare legs. Well, why not let Elizabeth keep her socks, to show that she is really only a baby, though she's getting on for eleven? You can easily explain that to Miss Thomas.'

'That's a good idea,' said Nora, with a laugh. 'All right, Elizabeth – keep your socks on, and we'll explain to everyone that we're letting you because you're really not much more than a baby!'

The girls went out of the room laughing. Elizabeth put on her bedspread and stood thinking. She didn't think she wanted to keep her socks on now! If only the younger children wore them, because they were the babies of the school, *she* didn't want to. The babies would laugh at her, and so would the others.

Elizabeth tore off her shoes, grabbed her socks and pulled them off in a temper. She took out her stockings and pulled them on. Bother, bother, bother! Now she would have to wear stockings after all!

She flew downstairs to the gym, where she had been told to go after making her bed and tidying her cubicle. All the others were there. Elizabeth had felt sure that they would all make remarks about her stockings being on after all – but nobody took any notice of her at all.

Hymns were sung and prayers said. Miss Best read part of a Bible chapter in her rather stern voice. Then she called the names of all the girls and boys to see that they were there.

Elizabeth had a good look round. The boys and girls were in separate rows. There were a good many masters and mistresses. The matron of the school, who looked after the children when they were ill, stood on the platform with some of the other mistresses, a fat, jolly-looking person, dressed like a nurse, in apron and cap. The music-master played the piano for the singing, and again when the children marched out.

He made up a fine marching tune, and Elizabeth liked it very much for she loved music. She wondered if she was supposed to learn music at Whyteleafe. Miss Scott had taught her at home, but Miss Scott was not musical and Elizabeth had not enjoyed her lessons at all.

Out marched the children to their classrooms. 'You are in Miss Ranger's class,' said Ruth, poking Elizabeth in the back. 'Come with me and I'll show you.'

Elizabeth followed Ruth. She came to a big sunny class-room, and into it poured six boys and nine girls, all about Elizabeth's age.

39

'Bags I this desk,' squealed Ruth. 'I like to be by the window!'

She put her things into the desk. The other children chose their desks too, but the new ones were told to wait till Miss Ranger came. Ruth sprang to hold the door open as soon as she heard Miss Ranger's rather loud voice down the passage.

In came Miss Ranger. 'Good morning, children!'

'Good morning, Miss Ranger,' said everyone but Elizabeth.

'All the old children can sit, but the new ones must stand whilst I give them their places,' said Miss Ranger. She gave Elizabeth a desk at the back. Elizabeth was glad. It would be a good place to be naughty in! She meant to be bad in class that very morning. The sooner that everyone knew how naughty she meant to be, the sooner she would be sent home.

Books were given out. 'We will take a reading lesson first,' said Miss Ranger, who wanted to make sure that the new children could read properly. 'Then Dictation – then Arithmetic!'

Elizabeth could read beautifully, spell well, and she liked arithmetic. She couldn't help feeling that it was rather fun to do lessons with a lot of people instead of by herself! When her turn came she read very nicely indeed, though she had a great many difficult words in her page.

'Very good, Elizabeth,' said Miss Ranger. 'Next, please.'

Elizabeth got all her dictation right. She thought it was very easy. Miss Ranger took a red pencil and marked 'VERY GOOD' on Elizabeth's page. Elizabeth looked at it proudly – and then she suddenly remembered that she had meant to be naughty!

'This won't do!' she said to herself. 'I can't get Very Goods like this – they'll never send me home. I'd better be naughty.'

She wondered what to do. She looked at Ruth by the window, and wondered if she could flip her rubber at her and hit her. She took her ruler, fitted her rubber against the end of it, bent it back and let it go. Whizzzzzz! The rubber flew across the schoolroom and hit Ruth on the left ear!

'Ooooh!' said Ruth, in surprise. She looked round and saw Elizabeth's grinning face. Others began to giggle when they saw Ruth's angry look.

Elizabeth grew bolder. She folded up a bit of paper, and flipped it at Helen, who sat in front. But Helen moved her head, and the pellet of paper flew past her and landed on Miss Ranger's desk. She looked up.

'Playtime is for things like this,' she said. 'Not lesson-time. Who did that?'

Elizabeth didn't answer. Miss Ranger looked up and down the rows. 'WHO DID THAT?' she said again. The boy next to Elizabeth poked her hard with his ruler.

'Own up!' he whispered. 'If you don't we'll all be kept in.'

So Elizabeth owned up. 'I did it,' she said.

'Well, Elizabeth, perhaps you would like to know that I don't allow behaviour like that in *my* class,' said Miss Ranger. 'Don't do it again.'

'I shall if I want to,' said Elizabeth. Everybody looked at her in amazement. Miss Ranger was surprised.

'You must be very bored with these lessons to want to flip paper about,' she said. 'Go outside the room and stay there till you feel it would bore you less to come back than to stand outside. I don't mind how long you stand there, but I do mind anybody being bored in my class. Now, children, get out your paint-boxes, please.'

There was a clatter as the desks were opened and paint-boxes were taken out. Elizabeth loved painting and was very good at it. She wanted to stay. She sat on in her desk and didn't move.

'Elizabeth! Go outside, please,' said Miss Ranger. There was no help for it then – up Elizabeth got and went outside the door.

'You may come back when you think you can really behave yourself, and not disturb my class,' said Miss Ranger.

It was very dull standing outside the door. Elizabeth wondered if she should wander away and have a swing. No – she might meet the Beauty and the Beast! Ha ha! She was being naughty all right!

But it *was* dull standing so long outside a door and hearing happy talking coming from inside, as the children painted blue and pink lupins that Miss Ranger had brought in. Elizabeth couldn't bear it any longer. She opened the door and went in.

'I can behave myself now,' she said, in a low voice to Miss Ranger. Miss Ranger nodded, without a smile.

'Take your place,' she said. 'There's no time for you to do any painting – you can do a few more sums!'

'Sums again!' thought Elizabeth angrily. 'Well – I'll just be bad as soon as ever I can think of something really naughty again!'

7   The first school Meeting

That evening, after tea, the first Meeting was held. The whole school attended it, and Miss Belle, Miss Best, and Mr Johns came too. They sat at the back and did not seem to be taking a great deal of notice of what was going on.

'But all the same, they never miss a word!' said Ruth to Belinda, who was feeling just a little scared of this first important Meeting.

The two Head Children of the school, a grave-looking girl called Rita, and a merry-eyed boy called William, sat at a large table in the gym, where the Meeting was held. They were the Judges. Twelve other children, six boys and six girls, big and small, sat round a table just in front of the two Judges. They were called the Jury. All the others sat on forms around.

At first Elizabeth had thought she would not go to the Meeting. Then she had felt rather curious about it, and decided to go just this one time. She had seen a notice on the notice-board that said, 'Please bring all the money you have,' and she had brought hers in her purse – though she was quite determined not to give it up if she were asked to do so.

All the children stood up when the two Judges and the two mistresses and master came into the room – all but Elizabeth! However she got up in a great hurry when she felt Ruth's hard fingers digging into her back to make her move! She glared round at Ruth, and was just going to speak angrily to her when there was the sound of a hammer being rapped on a table.

'Sit, please,' said one of the Judges. Everyone sat. Elizabeth saw that there was a wooden hammer or mallet on the table in front of the Judges, and also a large notebook and some sheets of paper. There was a large box as well, like a big money-box. It all looked important and exciting.

'The twelve children round the smaller table are the monitors,' whispered Helen to Elizabeth. 'They are chosen by us all every month.'

Elizabeth saw that Nora was at the Jury table, and so was the boy she had kicked the day before. She didn't know any of the others, except Eileen, the girl who had been kind to her yesterday.

The girl Judge rose in her seat and spoke clearly to the school. 'This is our first Meeting this term,' she said. 'We have very little to do today, because school only opened yesterday, but we must just make our Rules clear to the new children, and we must also take in the money. We do not need to choose new monitors because we elected those at the last Meeting of the Easter term. You see them at the Jury table. They will remain monitors for one month unless any Meeting decides to choose others instead. As you know, monitors are chosen for their common sense, their loyalty to the school and its ideas, and their good character. They *must* be obeyed, because you yourselves have chosen them.'

The girl Judge stopped and looked down at a paper she held, on which she had written notes to remind her of what she wanted to say. She looked round at the listening children.

'We have very few rules,' she said. 'One rule is that we place all the money we get into this box, and we draw from it two shillings a week each. The rest of the money is used to buy anything that any of you especially want – but you have to state at the weekly Meeting what you need the money for, and the Jury will decide if you may have it.'

One or two of the children clinked their money as if they would like to put it into the box at once. The Judges smiled. 'You'll be able to give your money in a minute,' said the girl Judge. 'Now, to go on with our Rules. The second rule is that if we have any complaint at all, we must bring it to the Meeting and announce it there, so that everyone may hear it, and decide what is to be done with it.

'Any bullying, unkindness, untruthfulness, disobedience may be brought before the Meeting, and we will decide what punishment shall be given. Please be sure you understand the difference between a real complaint and telling tales, because telling tales is also punished. If you are not sure of the difference, ask your monitor before you bring your complaint to the Meeting.'

The girl Judge sat down. The boy Judge got up, and beamed round the listening company. 'We will now take the money,' he said. 'After that we will hand out the two shillings to everyone, and then see if anybody wants extra this week. Thomas, take the box round, please.'

Elizabeth was quite sure she was *not* going to give up her money. She quickly pushed her purse under her and sat on it hard.

Thomas came round with the box. Money clinked into it – shillings and sixpences, half-crowns and even a ten-shilling note or two went into the big box.

The box came to Elizabeth. She passed it on without putting her money into it. But Thomas the monitor noticed it at once. 'Haven't you any money at all?' he asked.

Elizabeth pretended not to hear. Thomas said no more, but went on taking the box round. Elizabeth was pleased. 'I did what I wanted to them and they couldn't stop me!' she thought.

Thomas took the box up to the Judges. It was very heavy now. He put it on their table and said something to them in a low voice.

William, the boy Judge, rapped on his table with the hammer. Everyone stopped chattering.

'Elizabeth Allen did not put her money into the box,' he said. 'Elizabeth, have you no money?'

'Yes, I have,' answered Elizabeth defiantly. 'But I'm going to keep it.'

'Stand up when you speak to me,' ordered the Judge. Elizabeth felt Ruth's hard fingers poking her again and she stood up. Ruth saw the purse on the form, and quickly picked it up.

'Why do you want to keep your money to yourself?' asked William. 'Are you so very selfish?'

'No,' said Elizabeth. 'But I think it's a silly idea.'

'Listen,' said William patiently. 'In this school we don't like to think that some of us have heaps of money to spend and others have hardly any. We all get the same, and if you want anything extra you can always have it if the Meeting agrees.'

'Well, I'm not going to stay at this school very long,' said Elizabeth, in a rude, defiant voice. 'And I shall want some money to go home by train – so I'm not going to give it to *you*.'

There was a buzz of surprise and horror. The Judges

and the Jury stared at Elizabeth as if she was something very queer indeed.

The two Headmistresses and the Master looked up with great interest, wondering what the Judges would say. William and Rita spoke together in low voices. Then they banged on the table with the hammer. Everyone was silent at once.

William spoke in a grave voice. 'We think Elizabeth is wrong and silly,' he said. 'Her parents are paying a lot of money to keep her in this fine school, and even if she goes home in a short while, her term's fees still have to be paid. Also we think she is very feeble not to try and see if she likes Whyteleafe.'

'If I'm not sent home, I'll *run* away,' said Elizabeth, angry at being spoken of like this.

'That can't be allowed,' said William at once. 'You would worry your parents and everyone here, just because you are a selfish, silly girl. Ruth, is that Elizabeth's money I see you waving at me? Bring it here.'

Elizabeth made a snatch at her money, but it was too late. Ruth took the bag to the table and emptied six shillings, two half-crowns, and five sixpences into the money-box. Elizabeth blinked her eyes. She wanted to cry, but she wasn't going to.

'Elizabeth, we can't allow you to keep your money in case you are foolish enough to use it for running away,' said Rita, in a kind but stern voice.

One of the Jury stood up. It was a tall boy called Maurice. 'I should like to say that the Jury think that Elizabeth Allen must not have any money at all to spend this week, because of her behaviour,' he said.

All the Jury put up their hands to show that they agreed.

'Very well,' said the Judge. 'Now, Elizabeth, we shan't say any more to you today, because you are a new girl, and must be given a chance to settle down. I hope you will have a good report at next week's Meeting. We shall be very pleased if you do.'

'Well, I shan't, then,' said Elizabeth, in a furious voice. 'You just wait and see what I'll do.'

'Sit down,' said William, losing his patience with the defiant little girl. 'We've had enough of you for one meeting. Nora, give out the money to everyone, please.'

Nora gave two shillings to everybody, except Elizabeth. The little girl sat sulking on her form, hating everybody. How dared they take her money? She would pay Ruth out for taking her purse like that!

When everyone had their money, the Judges knocked for silence again. 'Does anyone want extra money this week for anything?' asked William.

A small boy stood up. 'I should like sixpence extra,' he said.

'What for?' asked William.

'I've been told I must give some money to the School Club, to help towards a new gramophone,' he said.

'Well, take it out of your two shillings,' said William. 'Sit down. Sixpence extra not granted.'

The boy sat down. A girl got up. 'May I have one and ninepence extra to pay for an electric light bulb I broke by accident in the playroom?' she asked.

'Who's your monitor?' asked Rita. One of the Jury stood up, a girl called Winnie.

'Was it a proper accident, Winnie, or just fooling about?' asked Rita.

'It was a proper accident,' said Winnie. 'Elsie was trying to open a tin, and the opener flew out of her hand and broke the light bulb.'

'Give her one and ninepence out of the box, then,' ordered Rita. Winnie took the money and gave it to the girl, who was very pleased.

'Any more requests?' asked William. Nobody said anything. 'Any complaints or grumbles?' asked Rita.

Elizabeth felt uncomfortable. Would Nora complain about her? Would that boy she had kicked, who was a monitor, complain too? Goodness, this Meeting was lasting much too long!

8   The first week at school

Nobody made any complaints at all. Elizabeth couldn't help feeling glad. 'All the same, they'll have plenty of complaints to make about me next week!' she thought. 'I'll just show them that I mean what I say!'

Somebody had a grumble. It was a small boy called Wilfred. He stood up, looking rather shy.

'I have a grumble,' he said.

'Go on, then,' said William, the Judge.

'Please,' he said, 'I learn music, and one of the times put down for my practice is half of cricket-time on Tuesday. Could I have it changed, because I do hate missing cricket.'

'Certainly,' said William. 'Mr Johns, do you think that could be changed?'

'I'll see to it,' said Mr Johns, from the back of the room. 'I'll speak to the music-master and have it put right for Wilfred.'

'Thank you,' said William and Wilfred together. There were no more grumbles. William hammered on the table.

'The Meeting is over,' he said. 'The next will be held at the same time on the same day next week. Everyone must attend.'

The children jumped up, talking loudly, and went out to their various tasks. Some had lessons to prepare for the next day. Some had pets to feed. Some wanted to practise cricket or tennis. Everyone seemed to have something to do.

All except Elizabeth. She seemed to have no one to talk to, no one to walk with. She knew it was her own fault, but she didn't like it. She wandered off by herself and came to a little room where someone was playing the piano softly and beautifully.

Elizabeth loved music with all her heart. She crept into the little music-room and sat down to listen. Mr Lewis, the music-master, was there, playing to himself. When he finished, he turned round and saw Eizabeth.

'Hallo!' he said. 'Did you like that?'

'Yes, I loved it,' said Elizabeth. 'It sounded to me like the sea.'

'It was supposed to be the sea on a summer's day,' said Mr Lewis. He was an old man, with gentle eyes and a small grey beard. 'It was written by a man who loved to put the sea into his music.'

'I wish I could learn to play it,' said Elizabeth. 'I really do wish I could. Am I supposed to be learning music at this school, do you know?'

'What's your name?' asked the music-master, taking out a small notebook and opening it. 'Mine is Mr Lewis.'

'Mine is Elizabeth Allen,' said Elizabeth.

'Yes – here's your name,' said Mr Lewis. 'You *are* down for music lessons with me. That's fine. We shall get on well together, and perhaps by the end of the term you will be able to play this sea-piece you like so much.'

'I'd like that,' said Elizabeth, 'but I shan't be here long. I hate school.'

'Dear me, what a pity,' said Mr Lewis. 'Most children simply love it – especially Whyteleafe School. Well, if you think you won't be here long perhaps I had better cross your name off my list. It seems a waste of time to have any music lessons if you mean to go.'

'Well – I might as well have one or two lesson,' said Elizabeth. 'I suppose I couldn't have one now, could I?'

Mr Lewis looked at his watch. 'Yes,' he said. 'I've got twenty minutes. Fetch your music and we'll see what you can do.'

Elizabeth was happy for the first time when she sat down at the piano with the music-master by her side. She played one of her favourite pieces. Mr Lewis jerked his foot in time to the music and nodded his head when she had finished.

'Yes, Elizabeth,' he said, pleased. 'You will be one of my best pupils. I must ask you to change your mind about leaving us soon – it will be a pleasure to me to teach you that sea-piece.'

Elizabeth felt pleased and proud. But she shook her

head. 'I'm afraid I shan't stay,' she said. 'They've taken my money away so that I can't run away, but I'm going to be so horrid that they'll have to *send* me away!'

'What a pity!' said Mr Lewis. He looked at his watch again. 'Play me something else,' he said. 'I've a little more time.'

At the end of the lesson Mr Lewis showed Elizabeth the name of the sea-piece he had played. 'There is a most beautiful gramophone record of it,' he said. 'Why don't you ask for some money to buy it at the next Meeting? Everyone would love the record in the playroom, and I know they haven't got it.'

'I'd love to get it,' said Elizabeth. 'Then I could hear it whenever I wanted to. But I know the Meeting wouldn't give *me* any money! Why, they've even not let me have the two shillings everyone else has.'

'Dear dear,' said Mr Lewis, smiling. 'You must really be a *very* bad little girl – and yet you play my piano like an angel!'

'Do I really?' said Elizabeth in delight – but the music-master had gone, leaving Elizabeth to put away her music and shut the piano.

Elizabeth soon found out that there were many pleasant things that the children of Whyteleafe were allowed to do. Every other day they were allowed to go down to the village in twos, to buy sweets, toys, books, and anything they wanted. They were also allowed to go to the cinema once a week, provided that they paid for themselves.

They could go riding every day, and this Elizabeth simply adored, for there were rolling hills and commons around the school, on which it was perfectly lovely to gallop. Elizabeth rode very well indeed, for she had had her own pony for years.

Then, on two evenings a week, the music-master gave a little concert to those children who really loved music. The concert was from half-past seven to eight, after supper, and Mr Lewis gathered round him about twelve boys and girls who loved to hear the beautiful music he drew from his piano. Sometimes he played the violin too, and Elizabeth longed to learn to play it when she heard Mr Lewis drawing the bow across the strings of his fine violin.

On another evening there was a small dance, beginning at half-past seven, for an hour. Elizabeth loved dancing too, and when she saw the notice on the notice-board, she was pleased.

No wonder the children were happy at Whyteleafe! There seemed always something lovely to look forward to, something exciting to do. Helen and Belinda, the other new girls, soon settled down well, made firm friends with one another, and were very happy. The two new boys also made friends. Once Joan tried to make friends with Elizabeth, but the little girl made a rude face and turned away.

As the days went on, Elizabeth kept to her plan. She took every chance of being naughty and rude, till everyone was tired of her. She spent most of the mornings outside the door of the classroom because Miss Ranger could not have her in the room as she disturbed the class so much.

One morning she caught the school cat and put it inside Miss Ranger's desk before anyone entered the room. When Miss Ranger opened the lid, the cat jumped out, and Miss Ranger squealed in fright. Everyone giggled. They knew it was Elizabeth, of course.

Another time Elizabeth put the classroom clock ten minutes fast, and Miss Ranger stopped the lesson too soon. When Miss Ranger found out, she was angry.

'As you all have missed ten minutes of your arithmetic lesson,' she said, 'I am going to give you two extra sums to do for your preparation time this afternoon.'

The class was angry with Elizabeth. 'You wait till the next Meeting!' said Ruth. 'There'll be some fine complaints about you there!'

'I don't care,' said Elizabeth. And she didn't.

One afternoon after tea Elizabeth wanted to go and see

the village of Whyteleafe. She went to Nora, her monitor, and asked her for permission to go and look at the shops in the village.

'Yes, you can go,' said Nora. 'But get someone to go with you. We are only allowed to go in twos.'

Elizabeth went to Ruth. 'Will you come with me to the village?' she asked. 'I want to look at the shops.'

'No thanks,' said Ruth. 'I don't want to go with anyone like *you*! I don't know how you might behave in the road. I might be ashamed of you.'

'I know how to behave in the road,' said Elizabeth crossly.

'Well, you don't know how to behave at school!' said Ruth, and walked away.

Elizabeth asked Belinda. But Belinda shook her head. 'I don't want to go,' she said.

Helen wouldn't go either, nor would Joan. Elizabeth didn't like to ask any of the boys, because they always laughed at her when they saw her coming.

'Here's the bold bad girl!' they said to one another. And soon poor Elizabeth began to be known as the Bold Bad Girl!

Elizabeth went back to Nora. 'Nobody will go with me,' she said.

'It serves you right,' said Nora. 'You can't go if nobody will go with you. We are not allowed to go alone.'

'Well, *I'm* going alone!' said Elizabeth to herself. And she slipped out of the school door, down the steps, round to the right, and through the big archway! Down the hill she ran to see the village.

She had a lovely time looking into all the shops. She looked longingly into the sweet-shop and wished she had some money to buy some toffee. She looked into a music-shop and wondered if they had the gramophone record of the sea-piece she loved. She looked into the toy-shop – and good gracious! Coming out of it was Rita, the Head Girl of Whyteleafe School!

Now what was naughty Elizabeth to do?

9 Rita has a job for Elizabeth

Elizabeth had no time to run away. Rita came out of the shop almost on top of her. She smiled at the little girl – and then she saw that she was alone. Her smile faded, and she looked stern.

'Surely somebody is with you?' she asked.

'No,' said Elizabeth.

'But, Elizabeth, you know by now that no one is allowed in the village by herself,' said Rita. 'You must always come with somebody. Why didn't you?'

'Because nobody would come with me,' said Elizabeth. 'I did ask a whole lot of them.'

'Well, you had better come with *me* now,' said Rita. 'I am alone, because the girls of the top class are allowed to shop by themselves. So walk along with me.'

Elizabeth was just going to say that she didn't want to, when she saw what lovely kind eyes Rita had. Rita was looking at her, and Elizabeth thought she was the kindest-looking girl she had ever seen – even nicer than Eileen. So she walked along by Rita in silence.

'You know, Elizabeth, it is strange that no one would go with you,' said Rita. 'Doesn't anybody at all like you?'

'No,' said Elizabeth. 'Don't you remember, Rita, that I told you I was going to be as horrid as could be so that I could go home? Well, everybody thinks I *am* very horrid, so nobody wants to talk to me or walk with me.'

'And are you *really* horrid?' asked Rita.

Elizabeth looked up. She was surprised that Rita should talk to her kindly, after having found her out in disobedience. But Rita did not look angry, only very understanding and wise.

Elizabeth thought for a moment. *Was* she really horrid? She remembered all the governesses she had had. She remembered that Miss Scott wouldn't stay with her. Perhaps she really and truly *was* a horrid girl.

'I don't know,' she said at last. 'I believe I am horrid really, Rita. I make myself horrider than I truly am – but all the same, I believe I can't be very nice.'

'Poor little Elizabeth!' said Rita. 'I wonder what has made you grow so horrid? You look such a nice little girl, and when you smile you are quite different. I do feel sorry for you.'

A lump suddenly came into Elizabeth's throat, and tears into her eyes. She blinked the tears away angrily. Now Rita would think she was a baby!

'Don't feel sorry for me,' she said. 'I *want* to be horrid, so that I can go home.'

'Couldn't you try to be nice for a change, and just give yourself a chance?' asked Rita.

'No,' said Elizabeth. 'I shan't be sent home if I am nice. I simply must be as bad as I can be.'

'But you will make yourself very unhappy,' said Rita. 'And you will make other people unhappy too.'

'Shall I?' said Elizabeth in surprise. 'Well, I don't mind making myself unhappy, if I can get what I want in the end – but I don't want to make other people unhappy. I think I *am* a horrid girl, but Rita, I wish you'd believe me when I say that I really don't mean to make the others unhappy.'

'Well, listen, Elizabeth,' said Rita, walking all the time back towards the school, 'there is someone in your room who isn't very happy. Have you noticed it? You might at least do what you can to make things nicer for her.'

'Who is it?' asked Elizabeth in surprise.

'It is Joan,' said Rita. 'She hasn't a happy home, and she comes back to school very miserable each term. She worries about her father and mother all the time, because they don't seem to want her or to love her. They never come to see her at half term.'

'Oh,' said Elizabeth, remembering that Joan usually did look rather sad. 'I didn't know.'

'Nobody knows except me,' said Rita. 'I live near Joan at home, so I know. I am telling you this, Elizabeth, because if you really *do* mean what you say about not wanting to make other people unhappy, you can just try to make things better for Joan. She hasn't any friend, any more than you have – but for a different reason. She is afraid of making friends in case anyone asks her to stay with them for the holidays – and she knows her mother wouldn't bother to ask any friend back to stay with Joan. And Joan is very proud, and can't bear to take kindnesses she can't return. Now – there's a job for you to do! Can you do it?'

'Oh yes, Rita,' said Elizabeth at once. Although she was spoilt, she had a tender heart, and when she saw that someone was in trouble, she would always go to help them. 'Thank you for telling me. I won't tell anyone else.'

'I know you won't,' said Rita. 'It *is* such a pity that you mean to be bad, Elizabeth, because I can see you would be splendid if you would give yourself a chance.'

Elizabeth frowned. 'It's no good,' she said. 'I'm going to do what I meant to do – get sent home as soon as ever I can. And I can't be sent home if I'm good.'

'Well, come and talk to me any time you think you would like to,' said Rita, as they walked in at the school gates. 'And I say, Elizabeth – don't go alone into the village again, will you? Can you promise that?'

Elizabeth was just going to say no, she wouldn't promise, when she thought of how kind and gentle Rita had been – and she felt she *must* promise.

'I promise, Rita,' she said, 'and – and thank you for being so nice. You make it rather difficult for me to be as horrid as I want to be.'

'*That's* a good thing!' said Rita, with a laugh, and the tall Head Girl walked away to her own room.

Nora met Elizabeth as she walked to the playroom. '*Did* you go to the village?' she asked.

'Yes, I did,' said Elizabeth.

'Who went with you?' asked Nora.

'Nobody,' answered Elizabeth defiantly.

'Then I shall report you at the next Meeting,' said Nora angrily.

'Report me all you like!' said Elizabeth, in a don't-care tone. '*I* shan't mind!'

'You'll mind all right when the time comes, Miss Don't-Care,' said Nora.

Elizabeth went to the playroom and put a record on the gramophone. She looked through the pile of records to see if the sea-piece was there that she loved. But it wasn't. She wondered how much it would cost. But what was the use of wondering that? She would never have any money now to buy anything! This horrid, horrid school!

Joan Townsend came into the playroom. People were used to her quiet ways, and nobody took much notice of her. They called her the Mouse, and often asked her where she kept her bit of cheese!

Elizabeth looked up and thought that Joan did indeed look very sad. 'Has the afternoon post come yet?' asked Joan.

'Yes,' said Helen. 'Long ago. Nothing for you, Joan.'

'Perhaps she hoped to hear from her mother or father,' thought Elizabeth. 'I hear from Mummy often, and Miss Scott has written twice – but I don't remember Joan getting a single letter!'

She was just going to say something to Joan when the supper-bell rang. The children all trooped into the dining-hall. Elizabeth tried to sit next to Joan but she couldn't. She noticed that Joan hardly ate anything.

After supper there was a concert in the music-master's room. Elizabeth ran up to Joan and spoke to her. 'Joan! Come and hear Mr Lewis playing tonight. He's going to play a lovely thing to us – my Mummy plays it at home, and I know it very well.'

'No thanks,' said Joan. 'I've got a letter to write.'

Elizabeth stared after her as Joan went to the playroom. Joan always seemed to be writing letters – but none ever came for her. Elizabeth ran to tell Mr Lewis she was coming to his little concert, and then she ran and peeped in at the playroom. Joan was there alone – but she was not writing letters.

She sat with her pen in her hand, and two big tears dropped on to the writing-pad on the desk below. Elizabeth was horrified. She hated to see anyone crying. She stepped into the room – but Joan turned and saw her coming. She wiped her tears away at once and spoke fiercely to Elizabeth.

'What are you spying on me for, you horrid thing? Can't you leave anybody alone? You're always making a nuisance of yourself.'

'Joan, I only wanted to . . .'

'Yes, I know what you wanted!' said Joan, just as fiercely. 'You wanted to see me crying, and then laugh at

me and tell all the others I'm a baby! You say you want to be as horrid and nasty as you can – but just you try telling the others you saw me crying!'

'Oh please, Joan! I wouldn't do that, I really wouldn't!' said Elizabeth, full of dismay to think that Joan should think such a thing of her. 'Joan, please listen . . . I'm not quite as horrid as I make myself be. Oh, do please let me be friends with you.'

'No,' said Joan, who was almost as obstinate as Elizabeth, when she was unhappy. 'Go away. Do you suppose I'd let the naughtiest girl in the school be my friend? I don't want *any* friend. Go away.'

Elizabeth went. She felt dreadful. How could she help Joan if Joan wouldn't believe that she was not quite as horrid as she pretended to be? She thought of Joan's unhappy, freckled face, and although the music-master played really beautifully that evening, for once Elizabeth did not listen in delight – for once she was thinking of somebody else, and not herself!

'If only Joan would let me help her,' thought Elizabeth. 'Rita wouldn't have told me if she hadn't thought I could do it. I wish I could have a chance of showing Rita I can really do something for somebody.'

Elizabeth's chance came that very night. When she and the other five girls in her room were in bed, and Elizabeth was almost asleep, she heard a sound from the end bed, where Joan slept. Joan was sobbing quietly under the clothes!

Elizabeth was out of bed at once, although she knew that the rule was that no one was to leave her own cubicle till morning. But Elizabeth didn't care for rules, anyhow – and she meant to go to Joan, even if Joan pushed her away as fiercely as before!

10 Joan's secret

Elizabeth slipped by Nora's bed, and by Belinda's. She came to Joan's, at the end beside the wall. She slipped in between the curtains and went to sit on Joan's bed.

Joan stopped crying at once and lay quite stiff and still, wondering who it was on her bed. Elizabeth whispered to her.

'Joan! It's me, Elizabeth. What's the matter? Are you unhappy?'

'Go away,' said Joan, in a fierce whisper.

'I shan't,' said Elizabeth. 'It makes me unhappy myself to hear you crying all alone. Are you homesick?'

'Go away,' said Joan, beginning to cry softly again.

'I tell you I shan't,' said Elizabeth. 'Listen, Joan. I'm unhappy too. I was so bad at home that no governesses would stay with me – so my mother had to send me away to school. But I love my Mummy, and I can't bear to be sent away from home like this. I want my dog – and my pony – and even my canary – so I do know how *you* feel if you are homesick.'

Joan listened in surprise. So that was why Elizabeth was so horrid – partly because she was unhappy too, and wanted to be at home.

'Now, Joan, tell me what's the matter with *you*,' begged Elizabeth. 'Please do. I won't laugh, you know that. I only want to help you.'

'There's nothing much the matter,' said Joan, wiping her eyes. 'It's only that – I don't think my mother and father love me – and I do love them *so* much. You see – they hardly ever write to me – and they never come to see me at half term – and it's my birthday this term, and everyone knows it – and I shan't get a present from them or a birthday cake or anything – I know I shan't. And it makes me feel so dreadful.'

'Oh, Joan !' said Elizabeth, and she took the girl's hand in hers and squeezed it. 'Oh, Joan. That's awful. When I think how my Mummy spoilt me – and gave me everything I wanted – and fussed me – and I was cross and impatient all the time ! And here are you, just longing for a little tiny bit of everything I had. I feel rather ashamed of myself.'

'Well, so you ought to be,' said Joan, sitting up. 'You don't know how lucky you are to be loved and fussed. Goodness ! I should be really thrilled and frightfully happy if my mother wrote to me even once a fortnight – and yours has sent you cards and letters almost every day. It makes me jealous.'

'Don't be jealous,' said Elizabeth, beginning to cry herself. 'I would share everything with you if I could, Joan; I really would.'

'Well, you can't be quite so horrid as everyone thinks you are, then,' said Joan.

'I think I am rather horrid, but I do make myself much worse,' said Elizabeth. 'You see, I mean to be sent back home as soon as possible.'

'That will make your mother very unhappy,' said Joan. 'It is a great disgrace to be expelled from school, sent away never to come back. You are very queer – you love your mother, and she loves you, and you want to go back to her – and yet you are willing to make her very unhappy. I don't understand you. I'd do anything in the world for my mother, and she doesn't love me at all. I try to make her proud of me. I do everything I can for her, but she doesn't seem to bother about me. *You're* as bad as you can be, and I expect your mother will love you all the same. It isn't fair.'

'No – it doesn't seem fair,' said Elizabeth, thinking hard. She was glad her mother wasn't like Joan's. She made up her mind to be very nice to her mother when she went back home, to make up for making her unhappy by her behaviour at school.

'You see, Elizabeth, the other girls see me waiting for letters every day, and they laugh at me behind my back, and think my parents must be very queer people,' said Joan. 'And I do hate that too. Last term I sent some letters to myself, just so that I should have some – but the others found out and teased me dreadfully.'

'It's a shame,' said Elizabeth. 'Joan, don't worry so. Perhaps things will come right. Couldn't we be friends, please? Just whilst I'm here. I don't mean to be here for long, but it would be nice to have somebody for a friend for a little while.'

'All right,' said Joan, and she took Elizabeth's hand. 'Thank you for coming to me tonight. I'm so glad you're not as horrid as I thought. I think you're *very* nice!'

Elizabeth slipped back to her own bed, her heart feeling warm and glad. It was good to have a friend. It was lovely to be thought very nice. No boy or girl had ever said that of Elizabeth before!

'I won't let the others laugh at Joan!' thought Elizabeth fiercely. 'She's my friend now! I shall look after her – she's just a timid mouse.'

To the astonishment of everyone the two girls soon became fast friends. They went down to the village together. Joan spent some of her two shillings on sweets, which she shared with Elizabeth. Elizabeth helped Joan with her sums during preparation in the afternoon, for Joan was bad at arithmetic and Elizabeth was quick.

Joan asked Elizabeth many questions about her father and mother. She was never tired of hearing how wonderful they were, and the presents they gave Elizabeth, and the fuss they made of her.

'What are they like to look at?' asked Joan.

'I could show you their photographs, but Nora locked them up in her box, by the window,' said Elizabeth.

'Well, fancy letting them stay there, when all you've got to do is to say you're sorry and that you know how to count,' said Joan, remembering what had happened. 'Goodness – I wouldn't let *my* mother's picture stay in that dirty old box!'

'I shan't apologize to Nora,' said Elizabeth sulkily. 'I don't like her – interfering creature.'

'She's not,' said Joan. 'She's a good sort. Sometimes I think you are an awful baby, Elizabeth. Only a baby would talk like that.'

'Oh! So you think I'm a baby, do you?' cried Elizabeth, flaring up in a rage, and tossing her curls over her shoulder. 'Well, I'll just show you!'

Nora was coming into the bedroom at that very moment. She was astonished to find Elizabeth flinging herself almost on top of her, shouting loudly : 'Nora! I'm sorry about those things you put in the box. I know how to count and I'll show you I can put six things on my chest-of-drawers.'

'Good gracious! Don't deafen me,' said Nora. 'All right – you can have them back.'

Nora unlocked the box, took out all Elizabeth's things, and gave them to her.

'You're an awful goose, you know,' she said, half-scolding, half-kindly. She had been pleased to see that Elizabeth had really tried to make friends with someone at last.

Elizabeth proudly put her photographs on her chest and showed them to Joan. The bell went for tea and they had to go downstairs before Elizabeth had finished saying all she wanted to. As they passed the hall letter-rack, Elizabeth glanced up to see if there were any letters for her.

'Goody! A letter from Mother – and one from Daddy too – and this looks like one from Granny!' said Elizabeth. She took them down. Joan had no letters at all.

'Hallo, Joan! Still glooming over the letter-rack as usual!' called Helen's voice. 'I'm sure I don't know what you'd do if ever you did find a letter there one day! Jump through the roof, I should think!'

Joan went red and turned away. Elizabeth saw that she was hurt, and she jumped round on Helen.

'I suppose you think you're funny!' she shouted. 'Well, perhaps you'd like to know that Joan had four letters and a card this morning, and she *didn't* jump through the roof. She's not quite such a cuckoo as you are!'

Helen was so astonished to hear Elizabeth sticking up for anyone that she couldn't say a word. Elizabeth made a rude face at her, tucked her arm through Joan's, and walked off with her.

Joan turned to Elizabeth. 'What an awful story you told!' she said. 'I didn't have any letters today and you know I didn't.'

'Yes, I know,' said Elizabeth. 'It *was* a story – but I really couldn't help it, Joan. You looked like a timid mouse that's been clawed at by a cat, and I felt like a dog that wanted to bark something horrid at the cat!'

Joan threw back her head and laughed. 'You do say the funniest things, Elizabeth!' she said. 'I never know what you will say or do next.'

Nobody ever did know what Elizabeth would take into her head to do or say. The days were slipping by now, and another week had almost gone. Elizabeth enjoyed her work, for she had a good brain and things came easily to her. She enjoyed the riding lessons, the gym, the painting, the walks, the concerts, and above all, her music lessons. She liked cricket, and she was getting quite good at tennis.

She had to keep reminding herself that she mustn't enjoy these things. She must really be naughty, or she wouldn't be sent home in disgrace. So every now and again she was very naughty indeed.

One morning she did every single thing wrong in her class. She wrote badly and spelt every word wrong. She got all her sums quite wrong. She spilt ink over her neat geography map. She whistled and hummed till she drove Miss Ranger quite mad.

Miss Ranger had been told to be patient with naughty Elizabeth, and she tried to be. But even the children became angry with her, although at first they giggled and laughed and thought she was funny.

'I shall report you at the Meeting tomorrow,' said a boy at last. He was a monitor, and had the right to report anyone. 'I'm sick of you. You disturb everyone.'

'And *I* shall report you too !' said Nora that afternoon. 'Three times you've not gone to bed at the right time this week. Last night you even came up later than I did ! And look at this – you've spilt ink over your blue bedside rug. That will have to be cleaned.'

'Well, *I'm* not going to clean it,' said Elizabeth rudely. 'I'll make it a bit worse, just for fun !' And the naughty little girl tipped up some more ink over another part of the rug.

Nora stared at her in disgust.

'You're too silly for words,' she said. 'Well, you'll be sorry at the Meeting tomorrow !'

'Pooh ! That's all *you* know !' said Elizabeth.

11   The Meeting punishes Elizabeth

The Meeting the next day was at the same time as before. All the children went, and once again the two Judges, Rita and William, sat at the big table, and the twelve monitors, the Jury, sat at the smaller table.

Other teachers were there too, this time, besides Miss Belle and Miss Best. They sometimes came to hear what was being done at the Meeting, although they never interfered.

Rita hammered on the table for quiet. Elizabeth sat looking sulky. She knew quite well that she would be scolded and punished, and she kept telling herself that she didn't care. But one week at Whyteleafe School had made her see that it really was a splendid school and she couldn't help feeling rather ashamed of her behaviour.

'Well, it can't be helped. They won't send me home unless I behave badly,' she kept saying to herself.

'Has anyone any more money to put into the Box?' asked William. He looked at a sheet of paper. 'Jill Kenton and Harry Wills have received money this week and have already put it in. Has anyone else any?'

Nobody had. 'Nora, give out the two shillings to every-one, please,' ordered William.

Nora began to give out the money. She even gave it to Elizabeth, who was most surprised. She had quite thought that, owing to her behaviour, she would get no money at all. She made up her mind to buy some peppermints and some toffee and share them with Joan. She whispered this to her friend, who was sitting beside her.

'Thank you,' whispered back Joan. 'I shall want most of my money to buy stamps this week, so I shall love to share your sweets!'

'Does anyone want extra money?' asked William. George got up and spoke.

'We need a new cricket ball for a practice game,' he said. 'We lost ours in the shrubbery.'

'You must look for it again before you get the money,' said William. 'Come to me tomorrow.'

George sat down. Queenie got up. 'Could I have some money to buy a birthday present for somebody?' she asked. 'It's my old nurse's birthday this week, and I'd like to send her something. Half a crown will do nicely.'

Half a crown was given to Queenie.

'I'd like a new garden spade,' said John Terry, standing up. 'I'm afraid it will cost rather a lot, though.'

Mr Warlow, the games master, got up and spoke for John.

'I should just like to say that in my opinion John deserves a new spade,' he said. 'He is the best gardener in the school, and I believe the peas we had for dinner today were due to his hard work.'

John's spade was passed at once. 'Give him the money,' said William. 'How much is it, John?'

'I'm afraid it is twelve shillings and sixpence,' said John. 'I've asked at three shops and the price is the same in each.'

Twelve shillings and sixpence was handed out. John sat down, blushing with pleasure.

Other things were asked for. Some were granted and some were refused. Then came the complaints and grumbles.

'Any reports or complaints?' asked Rita, knocking on the table for silence.

'I want to report Harry Dunn for cheating,' said a monitor firmly.

There was a buzz at once. Everyone knew Harry Dunn, a sly-faced boy in the class above Elizabeth's. He sat on his form, looking red.

'Cheating is awful!' said William, shocked. 'We haven't had a proper case of that here for three terms.'

'Don't give him any money to spend for the rest of the term!' called someone.

'No. That's a silly punishment for cheating,' said William at once. 'It wouldn't stop him and would only make him angry.'

There was a loud discussion about Harry. Rita banged on the table with her hammer.

'Quiet!' she said. 'I want to ask Harry something. Harry, what lesson do you cheat in?'

'Arithmetic,' said Harry sulkily.

'Why?' asked William.

'Well, I missed five weeks last term, and I got behind in my arithmetic,' said Harry. 'My father doesn't like me to be bad at arithmetic, and I knew I'd be almost bottom if I didn't cheat. So I thought I'd better cheat, and copy Humphrey's sums. That's all.'

'Yes – he did miss five weeks last term,' said a monitor. 'He had mumps, I remember.'

'And his father does get wild if he isn't near the top in arithmetic,' said another monitor.

'Well, it seems to me that we'd better ask Mr Johns if he'd be good enough to give Harry extra help in arithmetic this term, so that he can catch up what he missed,' said William. 'Then he won't need to cheat. Mr Johns, I can see you at the back this evening – do you think it would help Harry if you gave him extra time?'

'Rather!' said Mr Johns. 'I've already suggested it to Harry – and now that this has happened I think he'll be glad of extra help in arithmetic, won't you, Harry?'

'Yes, thank you, sir,' said Harry.

But William hadn't finished with Harry.

'We can't let you sit with the others in your class until we know you won't cheat again,' he said. 'You had better put your desk apart from the others until you have caught up with the arithmetic you've missed – and then you can go back, if you will come and tell me that you won't cheat again.'

'All right, William,' said Harry. He hated the idea of

69

being set apart because he was a cheat – and he made up his mind he would soon know as much as anyone else – and then he'd beat them with his own brains, and never cheat again.

'Cheating is only done by stupid or lazy people,' said William. 'Now – any more complaints?'

Then it was Elizabeth's turn to go red and look sulky! Up got Nora at once.

'I have a serious complaint to make,' she said. 'It is about Elizabeth Allen again. I am the monitor in her bedroom, and I can't make her go to bed at the right time. Not only that – she is awfully rude and horrid. I don't think she cares how she behaves at all.'

'I'll show you I've got good manners!' shouted Elizabeth.

'Yes – she has poured ink twice over her bedside rug, and refused to clean it,' said Nora.

'Well, we will send it to the cleaner's and Elizabeth can pay for it,' said Rita. 'It costs two shillings to get those rugs cleaned – so I am afraid you will have to give up your two shillings, Elizabeth.'

Elizabeth really didn't like to be rude to Rita. So she meekly took out her two shillings and passed them back to Nora, who put them into the money-box.

'About the going late to bed,' said William, 'that's easily dealt with. In future Elizabeth's bedtime will be altered, and she will go at half-past seven, instead of eight.'

'But I shall miss the concerts and the dancing,' said Elizabeth in dismay.

'That's your own fault,' said Rita sternly. 'If you are sensible, we will alter your bedtime next week – but *only* if you are sensible.'

'And now about the rudeness and horridness,' said William. 'I'm not sure we can blame Elizabeth for that. You know, we've usually found that rude children are caused by silly parents, who spoil them and let them say and do what they like. I should think Elizabeth's *parents* are to blame for her present rude behaviour. They haven't taught her good manners.'

Elizabeth leapt up at once, her face full of anger. 'Mummy and Daddy *have* taught me good manners!' she said. 'They've beautiful manners themselves, and Mummy is never rude to anyone.'

'Well, we shall only believe that when we see that you are following their example!' said William. 'Whenever you are rude this week we shall each say to ourselves: "Poor Elizabeth! She can't help it! She wasn't brought up properly!"'

'I'll show you I've got good manners!' shouted Elizabeth. 'I'll just show you, you horrid boy!'

Everyone began to laugh at the angry little girl. William banged on the table with his hammer. 'Silence! Elizabeth wants to show us that she has good manners. Go on, Elizabeth, shout a little more and call us names. Then we shall see exactly what your good manners are.'

Elizabeth sat down, boiling. So they thought her mother and father didn't know how to bring children up with good manners, did they? Well, nobody would be more polite than she would be, next week! They would have to say they were wrong!

Kenneth, the monitor in Elizabeth's class, got up next. 'Please, William and Rita,' he said, '*could* you do something about Elizabeth's behaviour in class? It is simply impossible. She spoils all our lessons, and we are getting very tired of it. I guess Miss Ranger is too.'

'This is really dreadful,' said Rita. 'I had no idea Elizabeth was so bad. I am very disappointed. Has *no*body a good word to say for her?'

No one spoke. No one said a word. And then everyone got a surprise, for up got Joan Townsend, the Mouse! She was blushing red, for she hated to speak in public.

'I – I – I should like to speak for Elizabeth,' she said. 'She can be very kind. She isn't really as horrid as she pretends to be.'

Joan sat down with a bump, as red as fire. Elizabeth looked at her gratefully. It was good to have a friend!

'Well, it's something to hear *that*!' said William. 'But it isn't enough. What are Elizabeth's favourite lessons?'

'Music, painting, and riding,' shouted Elizabeth's class.

'Well, Elizabeth, until you can behave in the lessons you don't seem to like, you must miss those you *do* like,' said William, after consulting with Rita for a while. 'You will miss riding, music, and painting this week, and you will not go down to the village at all. We hope there will be better reports next week, so that we can give you back the things you love. We simply can't let you spoil lessons for the rest of your class.'

Elizabeth could not stand the Meeting for one moment more. She stood up, pushed a chair aside, and rushed out. 'Let her go,' she heard Rita say, in a sorry sort of voice. 'She's being awfully silly – but she's really not as bad as she makes out!'

Poor Elizabeth! No money to spend – an early bedtime – no concerts, no dancing, no riding, painting, or music! The little girl sat on her bed and wept. She knew it was all her own fault, but it didn't make things any better. Oh when, when would she be able to leave this horrid school?

12 Elizabeth has a bad time

Joan went to find Elizabeth as soon as the Meeting was over. She guessed she would be in their bedroom. Elizabeth dried her eyes as soon as she heard Joan coming. She wasn't going to let anyone see her crying !

'Hallo !' said Joan. 'Come down to the playroom. It's raining or we could go and have a game of tennis.'

'Joan, it was decent of you to speak up for me,' said Elizabeth. 'Thanks awfully. But don't do it again, because, you see, I want *every*one to think I'm too bad for this school, so that I'll be sent home.'

'Oh, Elizabeth, do get that silly idea out of your head !' said Joan. 'I'm quite sure that the school won't send you home, and you'll only go on getting yourself into more and more trouble. Do be sensible.'

'Do you really think they won't send me home, how-*ever* badly I behave?' said Elizabeth in dismay. 'But surely no school would want to keep a really bad child?'

'Whyteleafe School has never expelled anyone yet,' said Joan. 'So I don't expect they'll start on *you*. You'll just have a perfectly horrid time, instead of having a lovely one. You'd have much more chance of going home if you went to Rita and said you'd be good if only she would do her best to get you home because you were so unhappy here.'

'Really?' said Elizabeth, astonished. 'Well, I didn't think of that. Perhaps I'll go to Rita. I'll see. I am really getting a bit tired of remembering to be bad. There are so many nice things to do here, that I can't help enjoying myself sometimes.'

'I think you're a silly goose,' said Joan. 'Come on down.

It will soon be seven o'clock, and you know you've got to go to bed directly after supper for a whole week, instead of at eight o'clock.'

Elizabeth frowned. 'I've a good mind to go at eight o'clock, just to spite them!' she said.

'Oh, don't be foolish,' said Joan. 'Do you suppose the Meeting cares if you go to bed at seven or eight? You'll only be hurting yourself, not anyone else, if you're silly.'

'Oh,' said Elizabeth, seeing for the first time that she was spoiling things for herself far more than she was spoiling them for other people. She sat and thought for a minute.

'Listen, Joan,' she said, 'I'll do as I'm told this week. See? I'll obey the orders of the Meeting, and go to bed early, and miss all the things I love – and at the end I'll go to Rita and tell her I'm so unhappy that I simply *must* go home, and I'll see what she says. I'm sure she could tell Miss Belle and Miss Best and they could write to Mummy for me.'

'Well, you do that,' said Joan, getting a bit tired of Elizabeth's curious ideas. 'Now do come on – bother – there's the supper-bell, and we've wasted all this time!'

They had supper – and then poor Elizabeth had to go straight upstairs to bed. Nora popped in to see that she had obeyed the orders of the Meeting and felt quite surprised to see Elizabeth under the sheets.

'Good gracious!' she said. 'You are learning to be sensible at last! Now just you listen to me, Elizabeth – the Meeting hates punishing anyone as much as they have punished you this week – so be good and sensible and obedient, and you'll find that everything will be all right at the next Meeting. By the way, I'll take up your bedside rug – the cleaner comes tomorrow, and I'll see that it's put ready for him to take.'

'Thank you, Nora,' said Elizabeth, in a very good voice.

The week that followed was not a pleasant one for Elizabeth. She had to see the others go out riding without her. She had to sit indoors and copy out sums instead of going out sketching with the painting class. Worst of all she had to tell Mr Lewis that she couldn't have her music lessons that week.

Mr Lewis was disappointed. 'Well, aren't you a little silly?' he said, patting her on the shoulder. 'What a pity! And we were going to do something rather exciting this week too – I've got Richard Watson to learn a duet, and I thought you and he could play it together. Duets are fun.'

'Oh dear,' said Elizabeth in dismay. 'I've never played a duet, and I've always thought it would be fun. Could you wait till next week, do you think, Mr Lewis? I might get all my punishments taken off by that time.'

'I should hope you *would*!' said the music-master. 'Now, Elizabeth, although you are going to miss your lessons with me this week, there is no need for you to miss your practice. Take this duet and try to learn your part by yourself – and next week I'll have Richard alone too, and we'll all have a go at it. Practise your other pieces too, and don't forget your scales.'

'I won't forget,' promised Elizabeth, and she ran off. Richard Watson was a big boy, and Elizabeth couldn't help feeling rather proud to think that Mr Lewis had chosen her to play a duet with him. She knew that Richard Watson played the piano and the violin beautifully.

Elizabeth turned over a new leaf that week. Nobody could have worked harder in class than she did. She only got one sum wrong the whole of the week. She didn't get a single mistake in dictation. Even the French mistress, Mademoiselle, was pleased with her because she learnt a French song so quickly.

'Ah, but you are a clever little girl!' she said to Elizabeth. 'Will you not help this poor little Joan to learn her piece? Always she makes mistakes, and is at the bottom of my class.'

'Yes, I'll help Joan,' said Elizabeth eagerly. 'I can easily teach her the song.'

'You have a good heart,' said Mademoiselle. Elizabeth went red with pleasure. The other children stared at her. They couldn't understand this strange girl who was so bad and horrid one week, and so good and helpful the next!

Elizabeth helped Joan to learn the song. She and Joan went off to a corner of the garden and Elizabeth sang each line of the song in her clear voice, and made Joan sing it after her. It wasn't long before Joan knew it perfectly.

'You are very decent to me, Elizabeth,' said Joan gratefully. 'I wish I was going to have a birthday cake on my birthday – I'd give you the biggest piece of all!'

'When is your birthday?' asked Elizabeth.

'It's in two weeks' time,' said Joan. 'And I do hate it so, because I know I shan't get a single card, and my parents are certain not to remember it. Everyone else seems to have a big cake, and presents and cards.'

'I think it's a shame,' said Elizabeth warmly. '*I* shall give you a present, anyhow – that is if only the Meeting will give me my two shillings! I shan't pour ink on my rug again, anyway – that was an awful waste of two shillings. I could have bought toffees with that. I haven't had a sweet for ages!'

'I'll buy some this afternoon and share them with you,' said Joan. 'I want most of my money for stamps, but I shall have a few pence over for sweets. It's a pity you can't go down to the village with me and choose the sweets. It would be fun to go together.'

'It would,' agreed Elizabeth. 'But I'm not going down till I'm allowed to. For one thing I promised Rita I wouldn't go alone – and for another thing, I'm jolly well not going to have the Meeting taking away my good times any more!'

They went indoors. On the way they met three of the boys, going out to practise bowling.

'Hallo, Bold Bad Girl!' said one of them. Elizabeth went red, and tried to rush at them. But Joan held her arm firmly.

'Don't take any notice,' she said. 'They only want to see you get angry – and after all, you do deserve the name, you know!'

The boys went off to the cricket field, grinning. Elizabeth felt very angry. She still had not got used to the good-natured teasing that went on all around her. She wished she could tease back, or laugh, as the other children did.

Miss Ranger was delighted with Elizabeth that week. The little girl really had a fine brain, and was fond of a joke. She could say clever things that made Miss Ranger and the class laugh heartily. She had only to look at a page once or twice and she knew it by heart! She liked her work and did everything well.

'Elizabeth, you are a lucky little girl,' said Miss Ranger. 'Lessons come easily to you, and you should be able to do something fine in the world when you grow up. Whyteleafe School and your parents will be proud of you one day.'

'Whyteleafe School won't,' said Elizabeth firmly. 'I shan't be here long enough. Half a term is as long as I shall stay, and I may go home before that.'

'Well, we'll see,' said Miss Ranger. 'Anyway, it is a

pleasant change to see the other side of you this week, and not the unpleasant rudeness of last week.'

Elizabeth practised hard at the piano all the week. She wanted to show Mr Lewis that she could play that duet with Richard ! Over and over she played the pages of the music, trying to get the right time, and to play softly and loudly at the proper moments.

One morning she got a letter from her mother enclosing some stamps. 'Now that you have to buy your own stamps I thought perhaps it would help you if I sent you some,' wrote her mother. 'Then you can spend all your money on the things you like.'

Elizabeth counted the stamps. There were twelve penny ones and twelve ha'penny ones. She divided them in half and went to find Joan.

'Joan ! Here are some stamps for you ! Now you needn't spend all your money on them,' said Elizabeth.

'Oh, thanks,' said Joan, delighted. 'What a bit of luck ! Your mother must be a darling to think of things like that. I'll go straight down and buy some toffee.'

She did – and the two girls sucked it happily after tea that day, as they wandered round the school garden. They came across John Terry busy gardening with his new spade. He showed it to the girls, and they admired it. Elizabeth told John about the garden she had at home.

'You sound as if you know a lot about gardening,' said John. 'Not many girls do. I suppose you wouldn't like to come and help me sometime, would you, Elizabeth? There's a lot to do, and in the summer-time not many people come and help.'

'I'd love to,' said Elizabeth proudly. Fancy clever John Terry asking her to help him ! 'I'll come whenever I can.'

'You do look happy, Elizabeth,' said Joan, staring at her friend's bright eyes. 'I don't believe you want to leave Whyteleafe at all.'

'Well, I do, then,' said Elizabeth, quite fiercely. 'I don't change my mind as quickly as all that ! You'll soon see. I'll ask Rita to get me sent back home before half-term !'

13　The third Meeting

The third Meeting came. Everyone went to the gym as
before, and took their places. Some of the teachers sat at
the back as usual. Rita and William came in last of all
and the children rose and stood until their two Judges sat
down.

Joan was sitting next to Elizabeth. She was hoping very
much that Elizabeth would not say anything silly, and so
spoil her week's good work and behaviour. Elizabeth
wished the Meeting was over. She was not used to having
her behaviour discussed and dealt with, and she didn't
like it at all. But she knew that everyone was treated the
same, and she saw that it was quite fair.

Money was put into the box. One girl, Eileen, had had
a whole pound sent to her by her grandmother, and she
put it into the box very proudly. She was glad to feel that
she could add so much to the spending money of the
school.

The two shillings were given out to everyone. Elizabeth
took hers gladly – now she would be able to buy some
sweets for Joan.

'Does anyone want anything extra this week?' asked
William, rattling the money-box.

Eileen wanted a shilling to get her watch mended, and
it was granted at once. Nobody else said anything.

'Nothing else?' asked Rita, looking round.

Elizabeth suddenly found herself standing up. 'I don't
expect you will let me have it,' she said, 'but I would very
much like something – it isn't only for myself, but it would
be nice for everyone else too.'

'What is it you want?' asked Rita.

'Well, there's a lovely sea-piece that Mr Lewis plays,' said Elizabeth eagerly. 'He says there is a beautiful gramophone record of it, and I *would* so much like it. I'm sure everybody would love it too. I know I could buy it with my two shillings, but I owe Joan Townsend a lot of sweets, and I'd like to buy her some this week.'

William and Rita looked at the twelve monitors below them at the small table. 'What do you think about it?' Rita asked them. 'You might discuss it for a moment.'

The jury discussed it for a few minutes. Then Nora stood up.

'We think the money might be granted to Elizabeth,' said Nora. 'We have heard her practising like anything every morning this week before breakfast, and we think she deserves a reward.'

'An extra two shillings is granted, then,' said William. 'Give the money to Elizabeth, Nora.'

Elizabeth was given another two shillings. She was really delighted. She thought the monitors were very decent to have granted her wish. She forgot that she had hated them all last week!

The Meeting passed on to complaints and reports. One boy, Peter, was reported for scribbling over one of the cloakroom walls.

'A disgusting habit!' said William severely. 'You will spend your next two playtimes cleaning off the scribble with soap and hot water, and then you will buy some yellow distemper from the school stores out of your two shillings, and repaint that bit of wall yourself. I shall come to see it at the end of the week.'

Peter sat down, very red. Never again in his life would he scribble on walls. He was not angry at his punishment for he knew that it was just – he must remove the mess he had made, and make the wall good.

'We *all* see the walls,' said William, 'and we certainly don't want to see your silly scribbles on them.'

Then there was a report on Harry, who had cheated the week before. Mr Johns had sent in a written note to

William about him. William read it to the Meeting.

'I have to report that Harry is rapidly catching up with the rest of his class in arithmetic,' wrote Mr Johns. 'After another week, he will be as good as the rest. As he will then have no reason to cheat, I propose that at the next Meeting Harry is told he may sit with the others again, and not apart.'

'What about letting Harry sit with the rest of his class *this* week?' asked one of the monitors. 'He's had a week of sitting apart, and it's not very nice.'

'No,' said William firmly. 'He cheated before because he didn't know as much as the others – and if we let him go back too soon, he'll be tempted to cheat again. We don't want it to become a habit. Harry, next week we hope to put you back in your old seat with the others.'

'Yes, William,' said Harry. He made up his mind to work so hard at his arithmetic that he would be top of the class before the end of the term – then the Meeting, and Mr Johns would know he had no reason to cheat at all!

'And now for the Bold Bad Girl, Elizabeth Allen,' said William. Everyone laughed. Elizabeth laughed too. It sounded funny, not horrid, when William called her by those names. 'Nora, what report have you to give?'

Nora stood up. 'An excellent report,' she said. 'Elizabeth has obeyed all the orders of last week's Meeting, and as far as I know has obeyed them cheerfully and well.'

'Thank you,' said Rita. Nora sat down. Rita opened a note. It was written by Miss Ranger.

'Here is a report to me from Miss Ranger,' said Rita. 'This is what she says: "It has been a pleasure to have a girl like Elizabeth in my class this week. She has worked well, could easily be top of her class, and has been very helpful to others who cannot work as quickly as she can. She has been as good this week as she was bad last week!"'

Rita looked up. She smiled her lovely smile at Elizabeth, and William smiled too.

'This is very good, Elizabeth,' said Rita. 'I too have noticed a great difference in you this week.'

'Have you?' asked Elizabeth, pleased to think that Rita had taken any notice of her. 'Rita, did you notice that my manners were better? Because I'd like you to think that my mother and father have taught me good manners and brought me up properly. I don't like people to think they haven't.'

'Well, we take back what we said about your parents being at fault,' said Rita. 'But you really must see, Elizabeth, that if a boy or girl is rude or horrid, it often means that their parents are to blame for not having taught them any better.'

'I do see that,' said Elizabeth. 'Well, you'll see my father and mother at half-term, and then you'll know that they couldn't possibly be nicer.'

'Oh – so you have made up your mind to stay with us, then?' asked Rita, with a sudden smile of amusement. She couldn't help liking Elizabeth, for the little girl said such funny things, and was so serious about everything.

'Oh no, I haven't,' said Elizabeth at once. 'But I see now that you wouldn't let me go home if I behave too badly – you'll only be angry with me and *make* me stay just to show me I can't get my own way. But, Rita, if I do try hard to be good, and do everything I ought to, will you please ask Miss Belle and Miss Best to let me go home? They can ask my parents at half-term to take me away. My mother wouldn't want me to stay anywhere where I was unhappy.'

William and Rita looked at Elizabeth in surprise, very puzzled to know what to do with such a strange little girl.

Rita spoke to William, and the jury discussed things together too. But nobody could decide anything at all. Rita hammered on the table and everyone was quiet.

'Well, Elizabeth,' said Rita, 'we simply don't know what to say to you. We've never been asked such a thing before. We think we'd better ask Miss Belle and Miss Best to help us. Please, Miss Belle and Miss Best, could you advise us what to do best for Elizabeth?'

The two headmistresses came up to the platform, and Rita got them chairs. Mr Johns came too, and sat with them. It was not often that the masters and mistresses came on to the platform at the weekly Meetings, and it seemed to make things much more important and serious.

'Well, first,' said Miss Belle, 'I think we should all discuss this thing together – and as it is not very pleasant to discuss a person when she is present, and Elizabeth may find it a little awkward to hear us, I suggest that she shall be given the chance to leave the room until we have finished. What do you think about it, Elizabeth?'

'I'd rather go out of the gym and wait till you say what's decided,' said Elizabeth. 'But please, Miss Belle, I shall be awfully naughty again if . . .'

'Don't say anything more, Elizabeth, my dear,' said Miss Best hurriedly. She didn't want the children to feel annoyed with Elizabeth. She knew it was very difficult to be fair if people were feeling angry.

Elizabeth went out of the gym. She went to a music-room nearby and began to practise her part of the duet. She hoped that she would be able to have her music lessons the next week, then she could play the piano with Richard.

The Meeting began to discuss Elizabeth and what to do with her. Everyone had a say, and everyone was listened to.

'We don't want her, she's a nuisance,' said one girl. 'Why not let her go?'

'We *do* want her,' said Miss Belle. 'I think we can help her a great deal.'

'She's been spoilt,' said William. 'It's always difficult for spoilt children to fit in anywhere. They think the world's made for them and them alone.'

'But you can't think how *kind* Elizabeth is really,' said Joan eagerly. 'I'm her only friend, and I know more about her than anyone. She really has a good heart. Mademoiselle said she had too.'

'That is quite true,' came Mademoiselle's voice from the back of the gym. 'This little Elizabeth is a good child at heart, and a clever one. But she is so-o-o-o-o obstinate.'

Everyone laughed at Mademoiselle's long 'so-o-o-o-o'.

'It's so silly to think that Elizabeth *can* be simply splendid, but means to be awful if we don't give her what she

85

wants,' said William. 'Fancy *wanting* to leave Whyteleafe School! I've never, never known anyone want to do *that* before.'

The discussion went on. Nobody could imagine how Elizabeth could want to leave such a fine school as Whyteleafe, where the children were so happy, and where they ruled themselves. Miss Belle, Miss Best, and Mr Johns smiled at one another when they heard the excited children blaming Elizabeth for wanting to leave Whyteleafe.

'I think I can see the answer to your problem,' said Miss Belle, at last. 'Shall we say this to Elizabeth – that she may certainly leave us after the half-term if she is really unhappy, and can say so honestly to the Meeting? She does not need to be rude or naughty or disobedient any more, but may be good, hard-working and enjoy herself all she likes – because we are *quite* willing to let her go, if she really wants to, in a few weeks' time!'

'Oh – I see,' said Rita, her eyes shining. 'You mean that Elizabeth can't possibly come and say she is unhappy, after enjoying herself at Whyteleafe till half-term! So she won't want to go after all – but we're offering her what she wants, so she needn't be bad any more?'

'That's right,' said Miss Belle. 'If Whyteleafe School is all you say it is, and I am very proud to hear it – then I think we can safely say that you children and the school will be able to keep Elizabeth here of her own free will. *We* shall see Elizabeth at her best – and we can all help her to be good and happy.'

Everyone stamped their feet and agreed. It seemed comical to them – they were going to tell Elizabeth she could leave when she wanted to – but when the time came they were sure she wouldn't want to! What a good idea! They all made up their minds to be as nice as possible to Elizabeth so that she simply *couldn't* say she was unhappy, when half-term came!

'Call Elizabeth in,' said Miss Best. 'We'll tell her.'

14 A lovely week

Elizabeth was called back to the gym by Nora. She stopped playing the piano and went back to her place in the gym.

She wondered what the Judges were going to say. They looked serious, but not angry. Rita knocked on the table.

'Quiet,' she ordered. 'Elizabeth, we have all discussed what you want us to do. And we have decided that if you come to us at the Meeting after half-term, and tell us honestly that you are unhappy here, and want to go home, Miss Belle and Miss Best will advise your parents to take you away.'

'Really!' said Elizabeth in delight. 'Oh, thank you, Rita. I *am* pleased. Now I don't need to be horrid and rude any more. I can wait till half-term, but I warn you that at the very first Meeting after that I shall ask to go home. I hate being at school.'

Elizabeth wondered why everyone roared with laughter when she said that. She looked round in surprise. Even Joan was laughing.

'Well, Elizabeth, that's settled, then,' said Rita. 'Please be as nice as you know very well how to be until half-term – and then, if you wish, you can certainly go home, if your parents will take you away.'

'I know they will, if I'm unhappy,' said Elizabeth. 'Thank you, Rita. I promise to be really good now.'

'Very well,' said William. 'All your punishments are lifted from now on. Your bedtime will be as before, at eight o'clock. You can take riding and painting and all your favourite lessons.'

'Good!' said Elizabeth, beaming. She felt very pleased

with herself. She had got what she wanted! She could go home at half-term!

'I'm glad it's not before then,' thought the little girl. 'I do want to learn that duet with Richard. And I want to give Joan a present for her birthday. And I want to do some more riding – oh yes, and buy that record too! How everyone will love to hear it when I first put it on.'

Elizabeth was very happy. She beamed round at everyone, not listening to anything else that was said at the Meeting. There was very little else to discuss, anyway, and very soon the gym was empty, and the children ran off to their various tasks or hobbies.

'Well, Elizabeth, I've got you till half-term, anyway!' said Joan, tucking her arm into Elizabeth's. 'That's something.'

'Well, make the most of me!' said Elizabeth with a laugh. 'For you won't have me afterwards. I jolly well mean to go back home to my pony, and my dog. I mean to show my parents that I just *won't* be sent away to school!'

A lovely week began for Elizabeth then. After supper that night there was a little dance, and the boys and girls had great fun. When eight o'clock struck Elizabeth and the others of her age went upstairs to bed, leaving the older ones to go on dancing.

The next day she and Joan went down to the village to buy sweets, and the gramophone record that Elizabeth wanted. The music-shop didn't have it, but they said they would send for it to the town over the hill, and get it for Elizabeth. They would send it up to the school for her.

Joan bought some chocolate and a book. Elizabeth bought some toffee, and two packets of lettuce seeds. She hadn't forgotten that she was going to help John Terry with his gardening! Dear me, what a lot of things there were to do!

'You can have the first lettuce that grows from these seeds,' she promised Joan.

'Well, you'll have to stay till the end of the term then,'

laughed Joan. 'Lettuces don't grow quite so quickly as
you think, Elizabeth.'

'Oh,' said Elizabeth, disappointed. 'Well – *you*'ll have
to cut the first lettuce then, after I'm gone. Have a toffee?'

It was fun to eat toffees and talk to a friend. It was fun
to feel the lettuce seeds rattling in their packets. It was
lovely to think of going riding that afternoon and having
a music lesson after tea. Perhaps Richard would be there,
and they would play their duet.

The riding lesson was glorious. Twelve boys and girls
were taken out on the hills by the riding master. Elizabeth
had been used to her pony and she rode well, enjoying
the jog-jog-jog, and sniffing the fresh early summer
breezes. This was much better fun than cantering along
on her old pony at home.

That afternoon the postman brought a parcel for Elizabeth. She undid it – and inside she found a large chocolate cake, sent to her by her Granny!

'Oh, I say! Look at this!' cried Elizabeth. 'We can all
share it at tea-time!'

'My word, Elizabeth, you're rather different from when
you first came!' said Nora, staring at the excited girl as
she put her cake into her tin in the playroom. 'You
wouldn't share a *thing* then!'

Elizabeth blushed. 'Don't remind me of that, Nora,'
she begged. 'I'm ashamed of it now. All I hope is that you
won't all say no when I offer you some of this cake!'

Well, nobody did say no! Elizabeth counted the number of people at her table – eleven. She cut the cake into
twelve pieces. They were very large. Elizabeth offered the
plate round and soon there were only two pieces left.

'Thanks, Elizabeth! Thanks, Elizabeth!' said everyone,
taking a piece. They were delighted to have it, because
by now everyone's tuck-box was empty, and no more
goodies had come yet from their homes, for no one had
had a birthday.

'Your Granny must be jolly generous!' said Nora. 'This
is the finest cake I've ever tasted.'

Elizabeth was proud and pleased. She took the plate to Miss Ranger and offered her one of the two pieces that remained on it. Miss Ranger took it and nodded.

'Thank you, Elizabeth,' she said. Then Elizabeth helped herself to the last piece and settled down happily to eat it. This was better than keeping everything to herself! It was lovely to share. She looked round at all the contented faces, and liked to see the girls and boys eating *her* cake.

'Miss Scott would be surprised at me,' thought Elizabeth suddenly. 'She wouldn't know me! What a horrid girl I must have seemed to her.'

After tea Elizabeth got her music and raced off to Mr Lewis. Richard was there too, a big, serious boy with long clever fingers. He meant to be a musician when he grew up. He looked at Elizabeth and didn't smile.

'I suppose he doesn't think girls can play at all,' thought Elizabeth. She was right. Richard was disgusted to find that he was expected to play a duet with a girl – and Elizabeth too, that Bold Bad Girl! What would *she* know of music?

They began. Elizabeth had practised so hard that she knew her part wonderfully well. She took the lower part, the bass, and Richard had the more difficult part, the treble, where the higher notes were.

I shall count the first few bars,' said Mr Lewis. 'Now – *one* two three four, *one* two three four, *one* two three four . . .'

He soon stopped, for the two children found their own time, and the duet went with a swing. Mr Lewis let them play it all the way through and then he smiled.

'Very good,' he said. 'You have a feeling for each other's playing. Now, Richard, wasn't I right when I said I had found someone you need not be afraid of playing with?'

But Richard was as obstinate in his way as Elizabeth was in hers. He looked at the little girl's flushed face and did not answer. Elizabeth was disappointed.

Mr Lewis laughed. 'Thank you, Richard,' he said. 'You

may go – but come back in half an hour's time, and I will give you your lesson then. I am going to give Elizabeth hers now. Can you manage to practise together sometimes?'

'I suppose so,' said Richard ungraciously.

'Well, don't if you don't want to!' said Elizabeth, flaring up. 'I play my part just as well as you play yours. You made two mistakes.'

'And you made three!' said Richard.

'Now this won't do,' said Mr Lewis, patting Richard on the back. 'You can choose which you would rather do, Richard – play the duet with Harry, or with Elizabeth. I can find someone else for her, you know – but she's the best, after you.'

'Well – I'll have Elizabeth,' said Richard. 'Harry plays the piano as if his fingers were a bunch of bananas.'

Elizabeth went off into a peal of laughter. It tickled her to think of a bunch of bananas playing the piano. Richard laughed too.

'I'll practise with Elizabeth, sir,' he said to Mr Lewis. 'She's really jolly good.'

Elizabeth glowed with pride, because Richard was one of the bigger boys. She settled down to her music lesson happily. Mr Lewis made her play over the duet with him, and pointed out places where she went wrong. Elizabeth used to get cross when Miss Scott pointed out her mistakes, but with Mr Lewis it was different. She thought he was very clever indeed, and she could listen all day long to his playing!

'I've ordered that gramophone record, Mr Lewis,' she said. 'The shop is getting it for me.'

'I'll come and hear it when it arrives,' promised Mr Lewis. 'Now let's get on with tackling the sea-piece on *our* piano, Elizabeth. You want to learn it, don't you – but it won't be easy. Perhaps you could play it for me at the school concert at the end of the term, if you're good enough.'

'Oh, I'd love to,' said Elizabeth, pleased, and then she

stopped and looked disappointed. 'Oh, but I can't. I forgot. I shall be going home at half-term.'

'Really?' said Mr Lewis, who knew all about it. 'Still being the Bold Bad Girl? Dear, dear, what a pity!'

'Isn't there a concert at half-term?' asked Elizabeth, her voice trembling.

'Afraid not,' said Mr Lewis. 'Come along – get on with your scales now. Don't worry about not being able to play that sea-piece. I can easily get someone else to learn it for me.'

'Let me learn it, anyhow,' said Elizabeth. 'Even if I can't play it for you at a concert, I can still learn it for myself, because I love it.'

'Good,' said Mr Lewis. 'All right. I'll play it for you now, and you must listen hard.'

So Elizabeth listened and was happy. She was happy all the day, and she couldn't help being surprised at herself.

'It *is* a nuisance!' thought funny Elizabeth. 'I really can't go about being happy like this – whatever shall I say to the Meeting at half-term?'

15 Two tricks – and a quarrel

The week slipped by quickly. Elizabeth practised her pieces, and loved her music-lessons. She and Richard practised their duet together, and had such fun that they asked Mr Lewis for an even harder piece.

'I'm glad you chose me to play with you instead of Harry,' said Elizabeth to Richard. 'I do love the way you play, Richard. You are as good as Mr Lewis.'

'No, I'm not,' said Richard. 'But some day I shall be far, far better, Elizabeth. Some day you will come to London to hear me play at a great big concert! And some day you will hear the music *I* make up, played all over the world!'

It didn't seem like boasting when Richard spoke like this. Elizabeth didn't mock at him or laugh at him. She believed him, and although he was sometimes very moody and bad-tempered she grew to like him very much.

'I always hated boys before,' thought Elizabeth, surprised at herself. 'I do seem to be changing. I'd better be careful, or I *will* be different when I leave here, just as Miss Scott said!'

So, to show that she really did still hate boys she played a trick on Harry. She knew that he would have to go to the music-room to fetch some music he had left behind. Elizabeth took a sponge, filled it so full of water that it dripped, and then, climbing on a chair, she balanced the wet sponge on the top of the door.

She arranged the sponge so that anyone who opened the door would move the sponge, which would at once drop down on to the surprised person's head!

Then Elizabeth hid in a cupboard in the passage outside, and waited for Harry. He soon came along, rushing to fetch his forgotten music before the bell rang. He pushed open the door – and down fell the sponge on top of his head, squelch, squash!

'Oooh!' said Harry, in the greatest astonishment. 'Whatever is it?'

He soon found out! He took the sponge off his neck and threw it down on the floor in a rage. '*Now* I've got to go and change my coat!' he said. 'Who did that?'

Nobody answered, of course. But as Harry knew quite well that people who set traps for others usually like to hide somewhere near to see what happens, he guessed that the joker was in the passage cupboard!

He stole up to the cupboard, and flung the door open. Inside was Elizabeth, trying her best not to laugh loudly. Her handkerchief was stuffed into her mouth and tears of laughter were trickling down her cheeks.

'Oh, it's *you*, is it?' said Harry, hauling her out. 'It's the Bold Bad Girl! Well, I'll just stuff this wet sponge down your neck, see!'

But he didn't have time to, because the bell rang and he had to run. 'I'll pay you out for that!' he yelled. But Elizabeth only laughed mockingly.

'I hate boys!' she shouted. 'They're silly! Ha ha! I tricked you properly, Harry!'

But Harry soon paid Elizabeth back for her trick. He waited until the painting class, and then, when Elizabeth was quite lost in her work, bending over her painting, he stole up behind her. In his hand was a large sheet of paper.

He neatly pinned it to Elizabeth's back. The little girl felt something and shook herself – but the paper was safely on, and she didn't know it. She went on with her painting.

Harry went back to his place, giggling. The class was nearly over, and if Miss Chester, the art mistress, did not notice what he had done, there was a good chance of Elizabeth going about with the paper on her back.

Everyone saw the paper and giggled. On it was printed

in big letters: 'I'M THE BOLD BAD GIRL! BE-WARE! I BARK! I BITE! I HATE EVERYBODY!'

Joan was not in that painting class or she would have told Elizabeth what Harry had done. All the others thought it was very funny, especially as Elizabeth was known as the Bold Bad Girl.

The bell rang. Everyone cleared up their things. Miss Chester began to prepare for the next class, and did not notice Elizabeth's paper. The children went out of the art-room, and went to their own classrooms.

Once in her classroom all the others there saw the paper; they nudged one another and giggled. Joan was holding the door for Miss Ranger to come in, and did not see what everyone was laughing at. Soon Elizabeth no-ticed that the class was giggling at her, and she grew red.

'What are you all laughing at?' she demanded angrily. 'Is my hair untidy? Have I a smudge on my nose?'

'No, Elizabeth,' answered everyone in a chorus.

Then Miss Ranger came in, and the class settled down to work. They worked hard until Break, when the school had fifteen minutes play out-of-doors, and could have biscuits and milk if they wished.

Harry looked to see if the paper was still on Elizabeth's back. It was! He ran round to all his friends, pointing it out. All the boys kept behind Elizabeth, reading the paper and giggling.

'She's the Bold Bad Girl,' they whispered. 'Look at the notice!'

Every time that poor Elizabeth turned round she found somebody behind her, giggling. She grew so furious that she called out she would slap anyone who giggled behind her again.

Joan came out at that moment, and Elizabeth called to her. 'Joan! What's the matter with everyone today? They keep going behind my back and giggling. I hate it!'

Joan knew more of the ways of children than Elizabeth did. She guessed at once that someone had pinned a notice to Elizabeth's back.

'Turn round,' she said. Elizabeth turned round, and Joan saw the notice: 'I'M THE BOLD BAD GIRL! BEWARE! I BARK! I BITE! I HATE EVERY-BODY!'

Joan couldn't help giggling herself. 'Oh, Elizabeth!' she said. 'Do look what you've been going round with all morning! It's too funny! No wonder everyone laughed.'

She unpinned the paper and showed it to Elizabeth. The little girl, who was not used to being teased, went red with rage. She tore the paper into half and faced the laughing children.

'Who pinned that on me?' she asked.

'I didn't, Bold Bad Girl!' shouted someone. Everybody laughed. Elizabeth stamped her foot.

'Look out!' cried John. 'She barks! She bites! She'll show her teeth next!'

'I suppose the person who pinned that on me doesn't *dare* to own up!' shouted Elizabeth.

'Oh yes, I dare!' grinned Harry, nearby. 'I pinned it on you, my dear girl – in return for the wet sponge!'

'*Don't* call me your dear girl!' cried Elizabeth in a rage. 'You're a hateful boy, and a cheat, cheat, cheat! How *dare* you pin a notice on me like that! Take that!'

The furious little girl slapped Harry hard in the face. The boy stepped back in surprise.

'Stop that,' commanded Nora, coming up at that minute. 'Elizabeth! That sort of behaviour won't do. Apologize to Harry. He's too much of a gentleman to slap you back, as you deserve.'

'I won't apologize,' cried Elizabeth. 'Nora, I want you to report Harry at the next Meeting – and if you don't I *shall*!'

'Come with me,' said Nora to Elizabeth. She saw that Elizabeth was really upset, and needed to be quietened. 'You can tell me about it in the playroom. There's nobody there.'

Holding the torn bits of paper in her hand Elizabeth followed Nora, trembling with anger. Nora made her sit down and tell her what had happened.

Elizabeth pieced the bits of paper together and Nora read what Harry had written. She stopped herself smiling, but she really thought it was very funny.

'And why did Harry play this trick on you?' asked Nora.

'Just because I played a trick on him!' said Elizabeth. 'I put a wet sponge on the music-room door and it fell down on his head!'

'And why shouldn't Harry play a trick on you, then, if you play tricks on him?' asked Nora. 'You know, you wet his coat, and he was late for his class because he had to change it. If you weren't quite so silly, Elizabeth, you would see that the joke he played on you was quite as funny as the one you played on him. After all, you *know* that we call you the Bold Bad Girl!'

'You're not to,' said Elizabeth.

'Well, we certainly shall if you go on behaving so fiercely,' said Nora.

'Will you report Harry at the Meeting?' said Elizabeth.

'Certainly not,' said Nora. 'We don't report jokes!'

'Then *I* shall report him!' said Elizabeth.

'Elizabeth, that would be telling tales, not reporting,' said Nora firmly. 'You mustn't do that. Don't spoil this good week of yours by being silly. And, you know, I really *should* report *you*!'

'Why?' asked Elizabeth defiantly.

'Because I heard you call Harry a cheat, and you slapped him hard,' said Nora. 'It is very mean to call him a cheat when you know he isn't now. We try to help one another at Whyteleafe, and it was hateful of you to remind Harry and everyone else of something he's ashamed of.'

Elizabeth went red. 'Yes,' she said. 'That *was* hateful of me. I wish I hadn't. And I wish I hadn't slapped Harry now. I knew he wouldn't slap me back. Oh, Nora – I really have tried to behave decently, and now I've spoilt it all!'

'No, you haven't,' said Nora, getting up, pleased that Elizabeth's temper had gone. 'Little things like this can always be put right. Harry is a good-tempered boy. Go and say you're sorry and he won't think any more about it.'

'I don't like saying I'm sorry,' said Elizabeth.

'Nobody does,' said Nora. 'But it's a little thing that makes a big difference. Go and try it, and see if I'm not right!'

16 An apology – and another Meeting

Elizabeth went to find Harry. She noticed that everyone turned away as she came, and she was sad.

'They were all so friendly to me,' she thought. 'And now I've been silly again, and they don't like me any more. I do wish I didn't lose my temper.'

She didn't want to say she was sorry. She felt sure Harry would say something horrid, or would laugh at her. All the same, Elizabeth was truly sorry that she had called Harry a cheat. It was most unfair when the boy was doing his best to make up for his cheating. And Elizabeth was just a little girl, although she did such funny things when she was in a rage.

Harry was playing with about eight other boys and girls in a corner of the garden. Elizabeth stopped and looked at them. They turned their backs on her. It was horrid.

'Harry!' she called.

'I don't want to speak to you,' said Harry.

'But Harry, I want to say something to you in private,' said Elizabeth, almost in tears.

'Say it in public, then, in front of everyone,' said Harry. 'It can't be anything important.'

'All right, then,' said Elizabeth, going up to the group of children. 'I've come to say I'm sorry for calling you a cheat, when I know you're not now – and – and I'm sorry for slapping you, Harry. Nora has explained things to me, and I feel different now.'

The children stared at her. They all knew how hard it was to apologize, especially in front of others, and they admired the little girl.

Harry went up to her. 'That's decent of you,' he said

warmly. 'You've got an awful temper, Elizabeth, but you're a good sort all the same.'

Everybody smiled. Everybody was friendly again. What a difference a little apology made! Elizabeth could hardly believe it. She suddenly felt that everything was perfectly all right, and she wanted to skip for joy.

'Come and see my rabbits,' said Harry, slipping his arm through Elizabeth's. 'I've got two, called Bubble and Squeak, and they've got three babies. Would you like one?'

Elizabeth had always longed for a rabbit. She stared at Harry in delight. 'Oh *yes!*' she said. 'Let me buy one from you.'

'No, I'll *give* you one,' said Harry, who was a very generous boy, and was eager to make Elizabeth forget all about the quarrel. 'I've got a little old hutch you can have for it. It will be ready to leave its mother about half-term.'

'Oh!' said Elizabeth, disappointed. 'I shan't be here after that. I shall be going home, you know. I can't have the rabbit!'

The bell rang for school again, so she couldn't see the baby rabbit. She didn't want to, now, either, because she wouldn't be able to have it. What a pity she couldn't have it now, and give it back to Harry at half-term!

She asked Harry and Richard to come and listen to the new gramophone record that evening. It had come, and was, as Mr Lewis said, very lovely. The three children sat and listened to it. They played it five times. They were all fond of music, and Harry played quite well although his fingers were, as Richard had said, rather like a bunch of bananas! But he couldn't help that!

'You know, Elizabeth, we have a marvellous concert at the end of the term,' said Harry, putting the record on for the sixth time, and letting the sea-piece flood the room again. 'It's a pity you won't be here for it. You could have played at it, and your parents would have been jolly proud of you.'

Elizabeth had a quick picture in her mind of herself

playing the lovely grand piano at the concert, and her mother and father sitting proudly to listen to her. For the first time she really wished she was staying on at Whyteleafe School.

'But it's no good,' she said to herself quickly. 'I've made up my mind, and that's that! I shan't stay a minute longer than half-term.'

After supper that night Mr Lewis gave one of his little concerts. About nine children were in the music-room listening, all music-lovers. Mr Lewis had asked Elizabeth to bring her new record for them all to hear, and the little girl proudly put it on Mr Lewis's fine gramophone.

It was such fun to sit around listening. When two of the children thanked Elizabeth for getting two shillings to buy such a fine record, Elizabeth nearly burst with pride and pleasure.

'It really is fun to share things,' she thought. 'I simply loved all the others listening to *my* record. How could I ever have thought it was horrid to share things? I didn't know much!'

Joan was not such a music-lover as Elizabeth was, but she came to the concerts to be with Elizabeth. Joan was much happier now that she had a friend – though, as she said, it was rather like being friends with a thunderstorm! You never quite knew what Elizabeth was going to do next.

Elizabeth looked forward to the next School Meeting. She knew now that it was the most important thing of the whole school week. She was beginning to see that each child was one of a big gathering, and that, because its behaviour brought good or ill to the school as a whole, each child must learn to do its best so that the whole school might run smoothly and happily.

This was a difficult thing for a spoilt only child to learn – but Elizabeth was not stupid, and she soon saw what a fine thing it was for the children to rule themselves and help each other. But she also saw that they would not be able to do this as well as they did, if they had not had excellent teachers, able to teach and guide the classes in the best way.

'I see why everyone is so proud of Whyteleafe School now,' said Elizabeth to herself. 'I'm beginning to feel proud of it myself!'

Elizabeth enjoyed the next Meeting very much. Nora had said that she had nothing bad to report of her, and so Elizabeth had nothing to fear. She sat listening to the reports, complaints, and grumbles, and beamed with delight when she heard that Harry had been second in his class in arithmetic, and was now to be allowed to sit with the others again.

'Thank you,' said Harry to William. 'I shall never in my life cheat again, William.'

'Good,' said William. Everyone knew that Harry meant what he said and they were as pleased about it as Harry himself. The boy was different to look at now, too – his sly face had gone, and his eyes looked straight at everyone. He and everyone else had seen and known his fault, and he and the whole school had conquered it – there was nothing to be ashamed of now!

There was a report that Peter had carefully cleaned and newly distempered the wall which he had spoilt by scribbling.

'See that you don't have to waste your two shillings on buying distemper again,' said William to Peter.

'I certainly won't,' said Peter heartily. He had had to go without his weekly visit to the cinema, and had missed all his sweets for a week. He wasn't going to let *that* happen again!

There was a complaint about a small girl called Doris. The monitor who complained of her was very angry.

She stood up and made her report. 'Doris has two guinea-pigs,' she said. 'And on two days last week she forgot to feed them. I think they ought to be taken away from her.'

'Oh no, please don't,' begged Doris, almost crying. 'I

do love them, really I do. I can't think how I came to forget, Rita. I've never forgotten before.'

'*Has* she ever forgotten before?' asked William.

'I don't think so,' answered the monitor, who had reported Doris.

'Then it was probably quite a mistake, which will never happen again,' said William. 'Doris, pets trust us completely for their food and water, and it is a terrible thing to forget about them. You must write out a card and pin it over your chest-of-drawers to remind you. Print on it: "Feed my guinea-pigs". Take it down after three weeks, and see that you remember without being reminded. If you forget again your guinea-pigs will be taken away and given to someone who will remember them.'

'I'll never forget again,' said small Doris, who was very much ashamed that everyone should know she had forgotten her beloved guinea-pigs.

Nora reported that Elizabeth was behaving well, and said no more. Another monitor complained that somebody had been picking and eating the peas out of the school garden.

But John Terry immediately got up and said that the boy who had taken the peas had gone to him, and had apologized and paid him a shilling for the peas he had eaten.

'Then we'll say no more about that,' said William.

When the Meeting was over, Elizabeth went out to the garden to see Harry's rabbits. Harry was not there and the little girl looked at the furry babies running round the big hutch.

As she was standing there looking, she suddenly remembered something. She had meant to ask for extra money at the Meeting – and she had forgotten!

And what was the extra money for? It was to buy Joan a nice birthday present! Now Elizabeth would have to save her two shillings and buy it with that. She was cross with herself, for she had meant to ask for half a crown to buy Joan a little red handbag she had seen in the draper's shop.

Joan had said nothing to anyone but Elizabeth about her coming birthday. She hoped no one would notice it, because she knew she would have no cake to share with her friends, and no presents or cards to show. She became a timid Mouse once more, as her birthday came near, ashamed because nobody ever remembered her.

But a surprise was coming to Joan! And, of course, it was that Bold Bad Girl, Elizabeth, who planned it!

17 Elizabeth has a secret

During the next week, a registered letter came for Elizabeth from her Uncle Rupert. She opened it – and stared in delight. There was a pound-note inside!

'Twenty shillings!' said Elizabeth, in surprise. 'Two hundred and forty pence! Ooooh! How kind of Uncle Rupert!'

She read her uncle's letter. He said that he had just heard that she had gone to school, and had sent her some money to buy some nice things to eat.

'A whole pound!' said Elizabeth, hardly believing her eyes. 'I can buy heaps of things with that! I can buy Joan a *lovely* present!'

She went off to her bedroom to put the money into her purse. Plans began to form in her mind – wonderful plans!

'Oh!' said Elizabeth, sitting on her bed, as she thought of the plans. 'What fun! I shall go down to the village – and order a fine birthday cake for Joan! She will think it comes from her mother, and she will be so pleased!'

Elizabeth went on thinking. 'And I shall order the new book that Joan wants, and send that through the post too – and I'll put a card in "With love from Mother!" Then Joan won't be unhappy any more.'

The little girl thought these were marvellous plans. She didn't stop to think that Joan would find out sooner or later that the cake and the book were *not* from her mother. She just longed to give her friend a fine surprise.

She couldn't ask Joan to come down to the village with her, in case Joan found out what she was doing. So she asked Belinda.

'All right,' said Belinda. 'I want to buy some stamps, so I'll go after tea with you. Don't spend your two shillings all at once, Elizabeth!'

All that day Elizabeth thought about the cake and the presents for Joan. She thought about them so much in the French class, that Mademoiselle got cross with her.

'Elizabeth! Three times I have asked you a question, and you sit there and smile and say nothing!' cried the French mistress, who was very short-tempered.

Elizabeth jumped. She hadn't heard the questions at all. 'What was it you asked me, Mam'zelle?' she asked.

This girl! She thinks she will make me repeat myself a hundred times!' cried Mademoiselle, wagging her hands about in the funny way she had. 'You will listen to me properly for the rest of the lesson, Elizabeth, or else you will come to me for an extra half-hour after tea.'

'Gracious!' thought Elizabeth, remembering that she wanted to go shopping after tea. 'I'd better stop dreaming and think of the French lesson.'

So for the rest of the lesson she did her best, and Mademoiselle smiled graciously at her. She liked Elizabeth, and found her very amusing, though she sometimes wanted to shake her when she said, 'Well, you see, Mam'zelle, you needn't bother about whether I shall be top or bottom in exams, because I'm not staying after half-term.'

'You are the most obstinate child I have ever seen,' Mademoiselle would say, and rap loudly on her desk, half angry and half smiling.

After tea Elizabeth went to get her money and to find Belinda. Helen said she would come too, so the three of them set off.

'What are you going to buy, Elizabeth?' asked Helen curiously.

'It's a secret,' said Elizabeth at once. 'I don't want you to come into the shops with me, if you don't mind, because I really have got some secrets today. It's to do with somebody else, that's why I can't tell you.'

'All right,' said Helen. 'Well, we are going to have

strawberry ice-creams in the sweet-shop. You can join us there when you have finished your shopping. Don't be too long.'

Helen and Belinda went off to the sweet-shop, and sat down at a little marble-topped table there to enjoy their ice-creams. Elizabeth disappeared into the baker's shop.

The baker's wife came to see what she wanted. 'Please, do you make birthday cakes?' asked Elizabeth.

'Yes, miss,' said the woman. 'They are two shillings and sixpence, five shillings, or, for a very big one with candles on, and the name, ten shillings.'

'Would the ten-shilling one be big enough for heaps of children?' asked Elizabeth, feeling certain that Joan would like to share the cake with everyone.

'It would be big enough for the whole school!' answered the woman, smiling. 'It's the size people often order for Whyteleafe School.'

'Oh, good,' said Elizabeth. 'Well, will you make a cake like that for Friday? Put eleven candles on it, all different colours – and put "A happy birthday for my darling Joan" on it. Will there be enough room for all that, do you think?'

'Oh yes,' said the woman. 'I'll decorate it with sugar flowers, and make it really beautiful, and it shall have two layers of thick cream inside.'

'I'll pay now,' said Elizabeth. 'Oh, and will you please send it to Miss Joan Townsend, Whyteleafe School, on Friday morning, early?'

'Any message inside, miss?' asked the baker's wife, writing down the name and address.

'No,' said Elizabeth. She took the pound-note out of her purse, and was just giving it to the shop woman, when Nora came into the shop. She smiled at Elizabeth. Then she looked round the shop. 'Are you alone?' she asked. 'Surely you didn't come down to the village by yourself?'

'Oh no, Nora,' said Elizabeth. 'I came with Helen and Belinda. They're waiting for me at the ice-cream shop.'

The little girl paid for the cake, and received ten shillings change. Nora stared at the money, and looked puzzled. Elizabeth waved goodbye and went out.

She went to the bookshop and ordered the book she knew Joan wanted. It was a book all about birds and cost five shillings. Elizabeth asked the shopman to send it by post, and to put inside a little card that she gave him. On the card she had written: 'With love, from Mother'.

'Now Joan will think her mother has sent her a fine cake *and* a present!' thought Elizabeth, pleased to think of Joan's surprise. 'I'll buy some birthday cards now.'

She bought three nice ones. In one she wrote 'With love, from Daddy', in the second she wrote 'With love, from Mother', and in the last she wrote 'With love, from Elizabeth', and added a row of kisses. She bought stamps for them, and put them safely in her pocket, ready to post on Thursday.

Then she went to buy the handbag she had seen in the

draper's shop. She had four shillings left by that time, so she bought the red bag, paid for a red comb and a red handkerchief to put inside, and put the change into the little purse belonging to the bag! There was sixpence change, and Elizabeth thought it would be fun to put that in too.

Then she went to the ice-cream shop. Helen and Belinda were there, tired of waiting for her.

'You *have* been a time, Elizabeth,' said Helen. 'Whatever have you been doing? You can't possibly be so long spending only two shillings!'

And then, for the first time, Elizabeth remembered that all money had to be put into the school money-box, and asked for! And she had spent a whole pound that afternoon, and hadn't even put a penny into the box.

She frowned. Goodness, now what was she to do? How *could* she have forgotten?

'Well, perhaps it's a good thing I *did* forget,' said Elizabeth to herself. 'If I'd put the money into the big money-box, and asked for a pound to spend on somebody's birthday, I'm sure Rita and William wouldn't have given me so much. It *is* an awful lot to spend all at once – but I did so want to give Joan a fine birthday!'

All the same, Elizabeth was rather worried about it. She had broken a rule – but she couldn't mend the broken rule because she had spent all the money! It was no use saying anything about it. The thing was done. And anyway Joan would have the finest surprise of her life!

But Elizabeth had a very nasty surprise on her way back to school with Helen and Belinda. Nora ran up to them and said, 'Elizabeth! I want to speak to you for a minute. Helen, you and Belinda can go on by yourselves. Elizabeth will catch you up.'

'What is it, Nora?' asked Elizabeth in surprise.

'Elizabeth, where did you get that money from that I saw you spending in the baker's shop?' asked Nora.

'My uncle sent it to me,' said Elizabeth, her heart sinking when she knew that Nora had seen the money.

'Well, you knew the rule,' said Nora. 'Why didn't you put it into the money-box? You knew you could have out what you wanted, if you really needed it for something.'

'I know, Nora,' said Elizabeth, in a small voice. 'But I forgot all about that till I'd spent the money. Really I did.'

'Spent *all* the money!' cried Nora in horror. 'What! A whole pound! Twenty shillings! Whatever did you spend it on?'

Elizabeth didn't answer. Nora grew angry. 'Elizabeth! You *must* tell me! Whatever could you have spent a whole pound on in such a little time? It's a real waste of money.'

'It wasn't,' said Elizabeth sulkily. 'Please don't ask me any more, Nora. I can't tell you what I spent the money on. It's a secret.'

'You're a very naughty girl,' said Nora. 'You break a rule – and spend all that money – and then won't tell me what you spent it on. Well – you can tell the next Meeting, if you won't tell *me*!'

'I shan't tell them,' said Elizabeth. 'It's a secret – and a secret I can't possibly tell. Oh dear! I always seem to be getting into trouble, and this time I really didn't mean to.'

Nora would not listen to any more. She sent Elizabeth to catch up Helen and Belinda. Poor Elizabeth! She simply did not know what to do. She couldn't tell her secret, because then she would have to own up that she was buying things for Joan, and pretending that they came from Joan's mother. And the Meeting would be angry with her just when she was being good and enjoying herself!

'Well – never mind – Joan will have a good birthday, anyhow,' said Elizabeth, thinking of the cake and the book. '*How* surprised she will be!'

18   Joan's wonderful birthday

'Joan, you will soon be eleven!' Elizabeth said at breakfast the next day, as she chopped the top off her boiled egg. 'Gracious! You *are* getting old.'

Joan went red and said nothing. She hated anyone to talk about her birthday, because she knew there would be no cards or present or cake for her. She was such a timid little mouse that she had no friends at all, except Elizabeth – and Joan was always feeling astonished that the bold Elizabeth should be *her* friend!

'I wonder if you'll have a cake?' went on Elizabeth, knowing perfectly well that Joan was going to, because she herself had ordered it! 'I wonder what it will be like?'

Joan scowled at Elizabeth. She really felt angry with her. 'How silly Elizabeth is, talking about my birthday, and if I'm going to have a cake, when she knows quite well that I don't want anything at all said about it,' thought Joan. She frowned at Elizabeth and signed to her to stop – but Elizabeth gaily went on talking.

'Let me see – it's Friday that's your birthday, isn't it, Joan? I wonder how many cards you'll have?'

'Joan didn't have a single one last year, and she didn't have a cake either,' said Kenneth. 'I don't believe she's got a father and mother.'

'Well, I have, then,' said Joan, feeling quite desperate.

'Funny they never come and see you, not even at half-term, then,' said Hilda, who liked to see Joan getting red.

'You be quiet,' said Elizabeth suddenly, seeing that things were going too far. 'What *I'm* surprised at is that *your* parents bother to come and see a girl like *you*,

Hilda! If I had a daughter like you, I'd go to the end of the world and stay there.'

'That's enough, Elizabeth,' said Nora, who pounced on Elizabeth very often since the little girl had refused to tell her her secret. Elizabeth said no more. She longed to say quite a lot, but she was learning to control her tongue now. Miss Scott would indeed not have known her!

Nothing more was said about Joan's birthday just then, and after breakfast, as the girls were making their beds, Joan went up to Elizabeth.

'Please, Elizabeth,' she said, 'for goodness' sake don't say any more about my birthday. You make things much worse if you do – think how I shall feel when everyone watches to see what cards and presents come for me by the post, and I haven't any! You are lucky – you have two Grannies, and two Grandpas, and Uncles and Aunts – but I haven't a single uncle, aunt, or granny! So it's no wonder I don't get many treats.'

'You *are* unlucky, Joan,' said Elizabeth, in surprise. 'Really you are. Well – I won't say any more about your birthday to the others, if you don't like it.'

But she longed to, all the same, for she kept hugging her delicious secret – Joan would have a wonderful cake, with eleven candles on, and cards, *and* presents too!

Nora was not kind to Elizabeth that week. She did not say any more to Elizabeth about her secret, but she had quite made up her mind to report her at the next Meeting. She thought Elizabeth was very deceitful and mean not to give up her money as everyone else did, and not to tell her what she had spent it on.

'After all, we gave her a fine chance to be as decent as possible, at the last Meeting,' said Nora to herself. 'We really did – and the funny thing is, *I* felt sure that Elizabeth would be worth that chance, and would do her best to keep our rules, and help the school, as we all try to do. But I was wrong. I don't feel as if I like Elizabeth a bit now.'

When Thursday came Elizabeth posted the three birthday cards she had bought. She could hardly go to sleep that night for thinking of Joan's pleasure in the morning! It really was lovely to give a surprise to someone.

Friday came. Elizabeth leapt out of bed, ran to Joan's bed, hugged her and cried, 'Many happy returns of the day, Joan! I hope you'll have a lovely birthday! Here's a little present for you from me!'

Joan took the parcel and undid it. When she saw the red handbag inside, she was delighted – and she was even more thrilled when she found the comb, the handkerchief, and the sixpence. She flung her arms round Elizabeth and squeezed her so hard that Elizabeth almost choked!

'Oh, thank you, Elizabeth!' she cried. 'It's perfectly lovely. I did so badly want a handbag. I only had that little old purse. Oh, how I shall love using it! It's the nicest present I have ever had.'

There was another surprise for Joan before she went down to breakfast. Hilda slipped into the bedroom with a lace-edged handkerchief for Joan. She had felt rather ashamed of herself for teasing Joan the day before, and had taken one of her best hankies to give for a present.

Joan was thrilled – in fact, she was *so* thrilled that a bright idea came into Elizabeth's head. She flew down to the playroom to see if Harry was there. He wasn't – but she could hear him practising in the music-room.

'Harry! Harry!' cried Elizabeth, rushing up to him, and startling him so much that his music fell to the floor. 'Will you do something for me?'

'Depends what it is,' said Harry, picking up his music.

'Harry, it's Joan Townsend's birthday,' said Elizabeth. 'You know you said you'd give me one of your rabbits, don't you, and I said it wasn't any good, because I was going at half-term – well, would you *please* give it to Joan instead, because you can't *think* how pleased she is to have presents!'

'Well—' said Harry, not quite sure about it.

'Go on, Harry, do say yes – be a sport!' begged Elizabeth, her blue eyes shining like stars. It was very difficult

to refuse Elizabeth anything when she looked like that.
Harry nodded.

'All right,' he said. 'What shall I do – bring the baby
rabbit in at breakfast-time?'

'Oooh!' said Elizabeth, with a squeak of delight. 'Yes!
Do! Say, "Shut your eyes, Joan, and feel what I've
brought you!" and then put it into her arms. What a
surprise for her!'

'Well, I'll go and get it now,' said Harry, putting his
music away. 'But she'll have to look after it herself, Elizabeth. It will be her rabbit.'

'I'll look after it for her,' said Elizabeth, feeling delighted at the thought of mothering a baby rabbit each
day. 'Hurry, Harry!'

Elizabeth went back to the bedroom. The breakfast-bell
rang as she was tidying her chest-of-drawers. She slipped
her arm through Joan's, and they went downstairs together. They stopped at the letter-rack. There was one
card for Elizabeth from Mrs Allen – and in Joan's place
were three envelopes, in which were the cards that Elizabeth had bought!

Joan took them down, going red with surprise. She
opened them. She took out the first card and read it:
'With love, from Mother'. She turned to Elizabeth, her
eyes shining.

'She's remembered my birthday!' she said to Elizabeth,
and her voice was very happy. She was even more surprised when she found a card marked 'With love from
Daddy', and she was delighted with Elizabeth's card.

'Fancy! Three cards!' said Joan, so happy that she
didn't notice that the writing on the envelopes was the
same for all three. She went into breakfast, quite delighted.

And on her chair was an enormous cardboard box from
the baker, and a small neat parcel from the bookshop;
Joan gave a cry of astonishment. 'More presents! Who
from, I wonder?'

She opened the little parcel first, and when she saw the
book about birds, and read the little card, her eyes filled

suddenly with tears. She turned away to hide them. 'Look,' she whispered to Elizabeth, 'it's from my mother. Isn't it lovely of her to remember my birthday! I didn't think she would!'

Joan was so happy to have the book, which she thought came from her mother, that she almost forgot to undo the box in which was the enormous birthday cake.

'Undo this box, quickly,' begged Elizabeth.

Joan cut the string. She took off the lid, and everyone crowded round to see what was inside. When they saw the beautiful cake, they shouted in delight.

'Joan! What a fine cake! Oooh! You *are* lucky!'

Joan was too astonished to say a word. She lifted the cake out of the box, on its silver board, and stood it on the breakfast-table. She stared at it as if it was a dream cake. She couldn't believe it was really true.

'I *say*!' said Nora. 'What a cake! Look at the candles – and the sugar roses! And look at the message on it – "A happy birthday for my darling Joan!" Your mother has been jolly generous, Joan – it's the biggest birthday cake I've seen.'

Joan stared at the message on the cake. She could hardly believe it. She felt so happy that she thought she would really have to burst. It was all so unexpected and so surprising.

Elizabeth was even happier – she looked at her friend's delighted face, and hugged herself for joy. She was glad she had spent all Uncle Rupert's pound on Joan. This was better than having a birthday herself – much, much better. Something that Miss Scott had often said to her flashed into her head.

'It is more blessed to give than to receive,' Miss Scott had said, when she had tried to make Elizabeth give some of her toys to the poor children at Christmas-time.

'And Miss Scott was quite right!' thought Elizabeth, in surprise. 'I'm getting more fun out of giving these things, than if I was receiving them myself!'

'Everybody in the school must share my birthday cake,'

said Joan in a happy, important voice, and she lifted her head proudly, and smiled around.

'Thanks, Joan! Many happy returns of the day!' shouted everybody. And then Harry came in and cried, 'Joan! Shut your eyes and feel what I've got for you!'

In amazement Joan shut her eyes – and the next moment the baby rabbit was in her arms. She gave a scream and opened her eyes again. She was so surprised that she didn't hold the rabbit tightly enough – and it leapt from her arms and scampered to the door, through which the teachers were just coming to breakfast.

The rabbit ran all round them, and the masters and mistresses stopped in astonishment.

'Is this a rabbit I see?' cried Mademoiselle, who was afraid of all small animals. 'Oh, these children! What will they bring to breakfast next?'

'I'm so sorry,' said Harry, catching the rabbit. 'You see, it's Joan's birthday, and I was giving her one of my rabbits.'

'I see,' said Miss Best. 'Well, take it out to the hutches now, Harry, and Joan can have it again after breakfast.'

'Oh, Elizabeth! I'm *so* happy!' whispered Joan, as they sat down to their eggs and bacon. 'I can't *tell* you how happy I am!'

'You needn't tell me,' said Elizabeth, laughing. 'I can see how happy you are – and I'm glad!'

19   Joan gets a shock

Joan had a wonderful birthday. She laughed and chattered in a way that no one had ever seen before. The little girl become quite pretty with happiness, and when she cut her birthday cake, and gave a piece to everyone in the school, her face was a picture!

'Nobody could possibly look happier,' thought Elizabeth, eating the delicious cake. 'Goodness! That baker certainly did make Joan's cake well. It's gorgeous!'

That evening, after supper, Elizabeth asked Joan to come and help her plant the lettuce seeds she had bought, but Joan shook her head.

'I can't,' she said. 'I'd love to, Elizabeth – but I've got something important to do.'

'What is it?' asked Elizabeth, rattling the seeds in her packets.

'Well – I've got to write and thank my mother and father for their cards, and the lovely cake and the book,' said Joan. 'I *must* do that tonight.'

'Oh,' said Elizabeth in dismay. She turned away biting her lip and frowning. 'Good gracious!' she thought. 'I didn't think of Joan writing to say thank you. Whatever will her mother think when she gets Joan's letter, thanking her for things she hasn't sent? Will she write and tell Joan she doesn't know anything about them – and what will poor Joan do then?'

Elizabeth went out to the garden, thinking hard. Now she *had* made a muddle! Why hadn't she thought of Joan writing to her mother? It was silly of her. Joan was going to be very unhappy – and perhaps angry – when she found out the truth.

'Perhaps it wasn't such a good idea after all,' said Elizabeth to herself. 'Bother! Why do I do things without thinking first? I wonder if Joan's mother will be angry with me for pretending those cards and the book and the cake were from Joan's parents. I don't feel happy about it any more. I feel dreadful.'

She went to give John Terry the seeds. He was delighted.

'Good!' he said. 'Just what I wanted. I plant a new row of lettuce every week, Elizabeth, and then we have new lettuces growing in different sizes, so that each week I have a fresh row to pull. Did you like the lettuces we had for tea yesterday? Those were out of the frames. I was rather proud of them.'

'They were simply lovely, John,' said Elizabeth, still busy thinking about Joan. She simply couldn't imagine what would happen and she felt worried.

She helped to plant the lettuce seeds, but John scolded her because she sowed them so thickly. 'I thought you knew something about gardening!' he said. 'Do you want the lettuces to come up like a forest?'

'Sorry, John,' said Elizabeth. 'I was thinking about something else.'

'You haven't been naughty, I hope?' asked John, who liked Elizabeth, and was always pleased when she came to help him in his garden. 'I hope you won't get ticked off at the Meeting again. You've had enough of that!'

'I'm afraid I *shall* be!' said Elizabeth, sighing. She was worried about that too – she was sure Nora would report her for spending a whole pound – and whatever would she say about it? She wasn't going to give away her secret, and let everyone know that it was she, and not Joan's parents, who had sent the cake and the book. Things were suddenly getting very difficult.

Joan was very happy for two days – and then she got a letter from her mother that took away all her happiness.

Elizabeth was with Joan when she found the letter at tea-time in the letter-rack. 'Oh! Mother has written very quickly to answer my letter,' said Joan happily, and she took the letter down. She tore it open and stood reading it.

Then she turned very pale and looked with wide, miserable eyes at Elizabeth.

'Mother says – Mother says – she didn't send me a card – she forgot,' said Joan in a trembling voice. 'And – and she says she didn't send me a cake – or that book – and she can't understand why I'm writing to thank her. Oh, Elizabeth!'

Elizabeth didn't know what to do or say. She put her arm round Joan and took her to the playroom. No one was there, for everyone had gone in to have tea. Joan sat down, still very white, and stared at Elizabeth.

'I don't understand it,' said poor Joan. 'Oh, Elizabeth – I was so very happy – and now I feel dreadful! Who could have sent those things – if it wasn't my mother?'

Still Elizabeth couldn't say a word. How could she say *she* had done it? Her kindness now seemed like a cruel trick. Poor Joan!

'Come in and have some tea,' said Elizabeth at last, finding her voice. 'You look so pale, Joan. Come and have some tea – it will do you good.'

But Joan shook her head. 'I'm not hungry. I couldn't eat *anything*,' she said. 'Let me alone. You go in to tea without me. I want to be alone – *please*, Elizabeth. You are kind and sweet to me, but I don't want anybody just now. I'm going out for a walk. I'll be better when I come back.'

Joan slipped out of the playroom. Elizabeth stared after her, unhappy and worried. Joan had gone out alone – without anyone, which wasn't allowed. Elizabeth simply didn't know *what* to do. So she went in to tea, very late, and was scolded by Nora.

'You're late, Elizabeth,' snapped Nora. 'You'll have to go without cake today.'

Elizabeth slipped into her place and said nothing. As she ate her tea, she noticed that the room was getting very dark indeed.

'There's a good old storm blowing up,' said Harry. 'My goodness – look at that rain!'

'Splendid!' said John. 'I badly need it for my broad beans and peas!'

But Elizabeth did not think it was splendid. She was thinking of poor Joan, out for a walk all alone in the storm. A roll of thunder sounded, and lightning flashed across the window.

'Joan hadn't even got a hat on,' said Elizabeth to herself. 'She'll be soaked! If only I knew which way she had gone I'd go and meet her with a mackintosh. Oh dear, everything's going wrong!'

She could hardly eat any tea. When the meal was over, she ran to the playroom and then to the bedroom to see if Joan was back. She wasn't. Elizabeth looked out of the window. She felt very ashamed and guilty.

'I meant to be so kind – and all I've done is to give Joan a dreadful shock, make her very unhappy, and now she's out in this dreadful thunderstorm!' thought Elizabeth.

For a whole hour Elizabeth watched for Joan to come back. The thunder gradually rolled itself away and the lightning stopped. But the heavy rain went on and on, lashing down on the new leaves of the trees, and making a noise like the waves breaking at sea.

At last Joan came back. Elizabeth saw a small dripping figure coming in through the garden-door. She rushed to Joan at once.

'Joan! You're simply soaked through! Come and change at once.'

Water dripped off Joan's dress, for the rain had been tremendous. The little girl was soaked through to the skin. She was shivering with cold.

'Oh, poor Joan,' said Elizabeth, dragging her friend upstairs. 'You'll catch a dreadful cold. Come on, you must change into dry things straight away.'

On the way up, the two girls met the matron of the school, who looked after them when they were ill, and who bandaged their arms and legs when they hurt themselves. She was a fat, jolly woman, and everyone liked her, though she could be very strict when she liked. She stopped when she saw Joan.

'Good gracious!' she said. 'Wherever have you been to get into that state, you silly child?'

'She's been out in the rain,' said Elizabeth. 'She's awfully cold, Matron. She's going to put on dry things.'

'I've got some of Joan's things airing in my hot cupboard,' said Matron. 'She'd better come along with me. Gracious, child, what a sight you look!'

Joan went with Matron. She was hurriedly stripped of her soaking clothes, and Matron rubbed her down well, with a rough towel. Joan said nothing at all, but stood looking so sad and miserable that Matron was worried.

'I think I'd better take your temperature,' she said. 'You don't look right to me. Put this warm dressing-gown round you for a minute. I'll get the thermometer.'

She sent Elizabeth away. The little girl went off to the music-room to practise, feeling very upset. She practised her scales steadily, and somehow it comforted her. She went to look for Joan at supper-time, but she was nowhere to be seen.

'Haven't you heard?' said Belinda. 'Joan's ill! She'd got a high temperature, and she's in bed in the San.'

The San., or sanatorium, was where any boy or girl was put when they were ill. It was a cheerful, sunny room, built apart from the school. So Joan was there, ill! Elizabeth's heart sank. She felt that it was all her fault.

'Cheer up! She'll be all right tomorrow, I expect,' said Belinda, seeing Elizabeth's dismayed face.

But Joan wasn't all right. She was worse! The doctor came and went with a grave face. It was dreadful.

'I know what would make Joan better,' thought Elizabeth, in despair. 'If only her mother could come and see her, and love her a bit – Joan would be quite all right! Her chill would go, and she'd be happy again.'

Elizabeth sat and wondered what she could do. Then an idea came into her head. She would write to Joan's mother! She would tell her of the presents she had given to Joan pretending that they were from Joan's mother. She would tell her how much Joan loved her mother, and wanted her to think of her and remember her – and she would beg her to come and see Joan because she was ill!

Elizabeth jumped up. She ran to Joan's writing-paper, which she kept on a shelf in the playroom. In it she found the letter from Joan's mother, and Elizabeth copied the address for herself. Then she slipped the letter back.

'Now I'll write to Mrs Townsend,' said the little girl. 'It will be the most difficult letter I've ever written – but it's got to be done. Oh dear – what an awful lot of trouble I'm going to get into!'

20 More trouble!

Elizabeth sat down to write to Joan's mother. She bit the
end of her pen. She began twice and tore the paper up. It
was very, very difficult.

It took her a long time to write the letter, but at last it
was done, and put in the box to be posted. This is what
Elizabeth had written :

'Dear Mrs Townsend,
I am Elizabeth Allen, Joan's friend. I am very fond
of Joan, but I have made her unhappy, and now she is ill.
I will tell you what I did.

'You see, Joan told me a lot about you, and how she
loved you, and she said she didn't think you loved her
very much because you hardly ever wrote to her, and you
didn't remember her birthdays. It is awful not to have
your birthday remembered at school, because most people
have cards and a cake. Well, I had a pound from my
Uncle Rupert, and I thought of a good idea. At least, I
thought it was a good idea, but it wasn't. I ordered a big
birthday cake for Joan, with a loving mesage on it – and
I got cards and wrote in them "With love, from Mother",
and "With love, from Daddy", and sent them. And I got
a book and pretended that was from you too.

'Well, Joan was awfully happy on her birthday because
she thought you had remembered her. You can't think
how happy she was. Then she wrote to thank *you* for the
things. I quite forgot she would do that – and of course
you wrote back to tell her that you hadn't sent them. Joan
got a dreadful shock, and she went out for a walk by her-

self and a thunderstorm came. She was soaked through, and now she is very ill.

'I am very unhappy about it, because I know it is all my fault. But I did really mean to make Joan happy. What I am writing for is to to ask you if you could come and see Joan, and make a fuss of her, because then I think she would be so glad that she would soon get better. I know you will be very angry with me, and I am very sorry.

'Elizabeth Allen'

That was Elizabeth's letter, written with many smudges because she had to stop and think what she wanted to say, and each time she stopped she smudged her letter. She licked the envelope, stamped it, and left it to be posted. What would Joan's mother say? If only she would come and see Joan and put things right for her; it would be lovely – but goodness, she would be very, very angry with Elizabeth!

Elizabeth missed Joan very much. The next day she went to ask Matron if she might see Joan, but Matron shook her head.

'No,' she said. 'The doctor says no one must see her. She is really ill.'

Elizabeth went to find John. He was putting sticks in for his peas to climb up. Every spare moment he spent in the school garden. That was the nice part of Whyteleafe School – if you had a love for something, you could make it your hobby and everything was done to help you.

'John,' said Elizabeth, 'Joan is ill. Do you think you could spare me some flowers for her?'

'Yes,' said John, standing up straight. 'You can pick some of those pink tulips if you like.'

'Oh, but they are your best ones, John,' said Elizabeth. 'Aren't you keeping them for something special?'

'Well, Joan's being ill is something special,' said John. 'Pick them with nice long stalks. Slit the stalks at the end before you put them into water – the tulips will last a long time then.'

Elizabeth just had time to pick the tulips, find a vase, and run to Matron with it before the school bell went. Matron promised to give the flowers to Joan. Elizabeth shot back to the classroom, and was only just in time.

'Don't forget it's the School Meeting tonight,' Belinda said to Elizabeth at the end of school that morning.

'Bother!' said Elizabeth in dismay. She had forgotten all about it. 'I don't think I'll come. I know I'm going to get into trouble.'

'You *must* come!' said Belinda, shocked. 'Are you afraid to?'

'No,' said Elizabeth fiercely. 'I'm *not* afraid to! I'll be there!'

And she was, sitting angrily on a form beside Harry and Helen, knowing perfectly well that Nora was going to report her as soon as possible.

'Well, if she does, I shan't give Joan's secret away,' thought Elizabeth. 'They can punish me all they like – but if they do I'll start being naughty again! Worse than ever!'

Of course Nora reported Elizabeth almost at once. She stood up and spoke gravely to Rita and William, the two Judges.

'I have a serious report to make,' said Nora. 'It is about Elizabeth. Although we gave her every chance to be good and helpful last week, I am sorry to say that she has been mean and deceitful. She went down to the village this week, and took with her a pound-note to spend, instead of putting it into the money-box to share out. She spent the whole pound and would not tell me anything about it.'

Everyone stared at Elizabeth in surprise.

'A *pound*!' said Rita. 'Twenty shillings – spent in one afternoon. Elizabeth, is this true?'

'Quite true,' said Elizabeth sulkily.

'Then it's too bad!' cried Eileen. 'We all put our money into the box and share it out – and we gave Elizabeth extra money for a record – but she puts *her* money into her own purse, the mean thing!'

Everybody thought the same. The children began to talk angrily. Elizabeth sat silent, looking red and sulky.

Rita hammered on the table. 'Quiet!' she said. Everyone was silent. Rita turned to Elizabeth. 'Stand up, Elizabeth,' she said. 'Please tell me what you spent the pound on – you can at least let us judge whether or not you spent the money well.'

'I can't tell you what I spent it on,' said Elizabeth, looking pleadingly at Rita. 'Don't ask me, Rita. It's a secret – and not my own secret, really. As a matter of fact, I quite forgot that I ought to put my money into the box, and then ask for what I wanted. I really *did* forget.'

'Do you think we would have allowed you to spend the money on what you bought?' asked Rita.

'I don't know,' said Elizabeth, rather miserably. 'All I know is that I wish I hadn't spent it on what I did! I was quite wrong.'

Rita felt sorry for Elizabeth. 'Well,' she said, 'you used the money wrongly and you know it – if you had only kept our rule, we should have known whether or not to let you have the money to spend as you did. Don't you see what a good idea our money-box is, Elizabeth?'

'Yes, I really do, Rita,' said Elizabeth, glad that Rita was speaking kindly to her.

'Well, now listen, Elizabeth,' said Rita, after talking with William for a while, 'we will be as fair as we can be to you about this, but you must trust us and tell us what you wanted the money for, first. If we think it was for a very good purpose, we shall say no more about it, but ask you to remember the rule another time.'

'That's very fair of you, Rita,' said Elizabeth, almost in tears. 'But I can't tell you. I know now that I did something wrong with the money – but there's somebody else mixed up in the secret, and I simply can't say any more.'

'Who is the other person in the secret?' asked Rita.

'I can't tell you that either,' said poor Elizabeth, who had no wish to bring Joan in. After all, it wasn't Joan's fault at all, that this had happened.

'Have you told anybody about this secret?' asked Rita.

'Yes, one person,' said Elizabeth. 'It's a grown-up, Rita.'

'What did the grown-up say when you told her?' asked William.

'She hasn't said anything yet,' said Elizabeth. 'I told her the secret in a letter, and she hasn't answered my letter yet. I only wrote it yesterday.'

William, Rita, and the monitors spoke together for a little while. Everyone was puzzled to know what to do. It was a very serious matter, and somehow it had to be dealt with.

'The Beauty and the Beast aren't here tonight,' said Nora, looking towards the back of the room. 'They are worried about Joan Townsend being ill. Only Miss Ranger and Mr Johns are here. If the others were here we could ask them for advice again – but somehow I feel I'd like to settle it without asking Miss Ranger or Mr Johns.'

'I think I know what we'll do,' said William at last. 'We'll leave the matter until Elizabeth has had an answer to her letter.'

'Good,' said Rita. She hammered on the table. 'Elizabeth,' she said, 'we are going to leave the matter until you have had an answer to your letter. Will you please come to me and tell me when you have?'

'Yes, Rita,' said Elizabeth gratefully. 'I think the person I wrote to will be very, very angry with me, and I wish I could tell you all about it, but I can't.'

'Well, it seems to me as if Elizabeth is being punished quite enough without us saying anything more,' said William. 'We'll leave it for a day or two. Then please go to Rita, Elizabeth, and tell her what answer you have received.'

Elizabeth sat down, glad that things were not worse. She thought the children were very fair and just. She hadn't even been punished !

When the two shillings were given out to everyone, Elizabeth put hers back into the box.

'I won't have it this week,' she said. 'I'll do without it.'

'Good girl,' said William. There was a nicer feeling in the room at once. Everyone felt that Elizabeth had tried to make up a bit for her mistake.

After the Meeting, Elizabeth went to ask how Joan was. The Matron came to the door of the San. and shook her head.

'She's not any better,' she said. 'She's worrying about something, the doctor says – and she even says she doesn't want to see her mother, though we have asked her if she would like us to send for her !'

'Oh,' said Elizabeth, and ran away in dismay. Now Joan didn't want to see her mother – and Elizabeth had written to ask her to come !

'I always seem to do the wrong thing !' said Elizabeth to herself. I wish I could go and tell Rita everything – then perhaps she could help me – but I can't do that without giving Joan away. She would hate to think that anyone knew her cake didn't come from her mother after all ! Oh dear ! Whatever *is* going to happen ? I wish Mrs Townsend would hurry up and write to me.'

21 Joan's mother arrives

Two days later Joan was seriously ill, and the Matron and doctor were very worried indeed.

'We must send for her mother,' said Miss Belle at once.

'The child begs us not to send for her,' said Matron in a puzzled voice. 'It is very strange. I hardly know whether it would be good for Joan to see her – she seems so much against having her mother sent for.'

'Well,' said Miss Best, 'the mother ought to come, for her own sake, if not for Joan's. She would be very angry if we did not send for her. We can tell her that Joan is behaving rather queerly about her. It may be her illness that is making her think funny thoughts.'

But Mrs Townsend arrived before she was sent for! She had received Elizabeth's queer letter, and had packed a bag, and taken a train to Whyteleafe the same day.

Elizabeth saw the taxi coming up through the archway of the school wall, but she did not know that Mrs Townsend was inside it. She did not see her get out, pay the man, and ring the bell.

Mrs Townsend was shown into the headmistresses' drawing-room at once. Miss Belle and Miss Best were most astonished to see her.

'I've come about Joan,' said Mrs Townsend. She was a small, sad-looking woman, beautifully dressed, and with large eyes just like Joan's. 'How is she?'

'Not any better, I'm afraid,' answered Miss Belle. 'But how did you know she was ill?' she asked in surprise.

'I had a letter from a girl called Elizabeth Allen,' said Mrs Townsend. 'A very queer letter – about Joan's birthday. Did she tell you anything about it?'

'No,' said Miss Belle, even more surprised. 'I know nothing about it. May we see the letter?'

Mrs Townsend gave the two mistresses Elizabeth's smudgy letter. They read it in silence.

'So that is what Elizabeth wanted the money for!' said Miss Best, her lovely smile showing for a moment. 'Well! Children **are** always surprising – but Elizabeth is the most astonishing child we have ever had – so naughty and yet so good – so defiant, and yet so kindhearted and just!'

'I understand now why Joan keeps saying that she doesn't want you to be sent for, Mrs Townsend,' said Miss Belle. 'She is ashamed, poor child, because she thought *you* had sent her those presents – and now she finds you didn't – and she is bewildered and hurt.'

'I think perhaps I ought to explain a few things to you,' said Mrs Townsend. 'I must explain them to Joan too.'

'Yes, please tell us anything that will help us with Joan,' said Miss Best.

'Well,' said Joan's mother, 'Joan had a twin, a boy called Michael. He was the finest, loveliest boy you ever saw, Miss Best. His father and I couldn't help loving him more than we loved Joan, because we both wanted a boy, and we didn't care much for girls. He was brave and bonny and always laughing – but Joan was always rather a coward, and beside Michael she seemed sulky and selfish.'

'Don't you think that might have been because you made such a fuss of the boy, and perhaps rather left Joan out?' asked Miss Belle. 'She may have been jealous, and that does queer things to a child.'

'Yes – you may be right,' said Mrs Townsend. 'Well – when they were three, both children fell ill – and Michael died. And because we loved him so much, we both wished that – that . . .'

'That Joan had been taken and Michael had been left to you?' said Miss Best gently. 'Yes, I understand, Mrs Townsend – but you did a great wrong to poor Joan. You have never forgiven her for being the only child left. Does Joan know she had a twin?'

'She soon forgot,' said Mrs Townsend, 'and we didn't tell her as she grew older. I don't think she knows even now that she ever had a brother.'

'Well, Mrs Townsend, I think you should tell Joan this,' said Miss Best firmly. 'She loves you very much and is miserable because she can't understand why you don't seem to love her.

'I *do* love her,' said Mrs Townsend. 'But somehow it is difficult to show it to Joan. When I got this queer little letter, telling me how somebody tried to buy Joan presents, pretending to be me, I felt dreadful. I felt I must come and see my poor little Joan at once.'

'Come and see her now,' said Miss Belle. 'Tell her what you have told us. Joan will understand, and once she is sure of your love, she will not mind how little you show it!

But it shouldn't be difficult to love a child like Joan – she she is so gentle and kind.'

'And what about Elizabeth?' asked Mrs Townsend. 'I must speak to her. I think she must be a very kind child, to try to make Joan happy.'

'Go and see Joan first,' said Miss Best. So Mrs Townsend was taken to the San. She opened the door and Matron beckoned her in, seeing at once that she was Joan's mother.

'She's asleep,' she whispered. 'Come over here and sit by the bed till she wakes.'

Mrs Townsend sat beside the bed. She looked at Joan. The little girl was thin and pale, and her sleeping face was so unhappy that her mother couldn't bear it. She leant over Joan and kissed her gently on the cheek.

Joan awoke and stared up. Her large eyes grew larger as she saw her mother. She looked at her for a moment and then spoke. 'Are you really here? Was it you who kissed me?'

'Of course,' said Mrs Townsend, with tears in her eyes. 'Poor little Joan! I was so sorry to hear you were ill.'

Joan's mother put her arms round her little girl and hugged her. Joan flung her arms round her mother's neck in delight.

'Oh, Mother! I didn't want you to come! But now I'm so happy!'

'I'm sorry I didn't remember your birthday, darling,' said Mrs Townsend. 'I think we've got a few things to say to one another. Why didn't you want me to come?'

'Because – because – oh, because I didn't think you would be pleased that somebody pretended to be you and sent me things,' said Joan. 'I was afraid of seeing you.'

'Now listen, Joan; I want to tell you something,' said Mrs Townsend, sitting on the bed and cuddling Joan beside her. And she began to tell the little girl of her lost brother. 'You see, I grieved so much for him, that I almost forgot I had a little daughter to make up for him,' said Mrs Townsend in a trembling voice. 'You have always been so quiet and timid, too, Joan – you never asked for things, never pushed yourself forward. So I never knew that you minded so much. You didn't say a word.'

'I couldn't,' said Joan. 'But I'm very happy now, Mother. This is the biggest surprise of my life. I understand things now! I do wish you had told me before. But it doesn't matter. Nothing matters now that I've got you close beside me, and I know you really do love me, and won't forget me again.'

'I will never forget you,' said Mrs Townsend. 'I didn't think you minded at all – but now that I know what you have been thinking, I shall be the kind of mother you want. But you must hurry up and get better, mustn't you?'

'Oh, I feel much, much better already,' said Joan. And indeed she looked quite different. When Matron came in, she was surprised to see such a happy-looking child.

'I shall want lots of dinner today!' said Joan. 'Because Mother is going to have it with me, Matron, and she wants to see how much I can eat!'

As they were eating their dinner together they talked about Elizabeth. 'I guessed that it was Elizabeth who sent those things, when you said it wasn't you,' said Joan. 'It was just the sort of mad, kind thing she *would* do! You know, Mother, she's the first real friend I've had, and *I* think she's splendid, though the first weeks she was here she was really the naughtiest, rudest girl in the school. The sad thing is – she's made up her mind to go at half-term, so I shan't have her very much longer.'

'I want to see Elizabeth,' said Mrs Townsend. 'She wrote me such a funny, sad letter. If it hadn't been for her letter, and what she did for your birthday, we shouldn't have come to understand one another as we now do, Joan! And although she thinks she did a very wrong thing, somehow or other it has come right, because she really did mean to be kind.'

'Matron! Do you think Elizabeth might come and see me whilst my mother is here?' asked Joan, when Matron came in to take her temperature.

'We'll see what your temperature is doing,' said Matron, pleased to see the empty plates. She slipped the thermometer into Joan's mouth. She waited a minute and then took it out again.

'Good gracious! Just below normal!' she said. 'You *are* getting better quickly! Yes – I think Elizabeth might come. I'll send for her.'

Elizabeth was practising her duet with Richard when the message came. One of the school maids brought it.

'Mrs Townsend is in the San. with Joan and says she would like to see you,' said the maid. 'Matron says you can go for twenty minutes.'

Elizabeth's heart sank. So Mrs Townsend had come to the school! She had got her letter – and now she was here, and wanted to see Elizabeth!

'I don't want to go to the San.,' said Elizabeth. 'Oh dear – isn't there any excuse I can make?'

'But I thought Joan was your friend?' said Richard in surprise.

'She is,' said Elizabeth, 'but you see – oh dear, I can't possibly explain. Things have just gone wrong, that's all.'

The little girl put her music away, looking glum. 'Cheer up!' said Richard. 'Things aren't so bad when you go and face them properly!'

'Well, I'll face them all right,' said Elizabeth, throwing her curls back. 'I wonder what's going to happen to me *now*?'

22 Rita talks to Elizabeth

Elizabeth went to the San. Matron was just coming out, smiling.

'How is Joan now?' asked Elizabeth.

'*Much* better!' said Matron. 'We shall soon have her out and about again now.'

'Oh, good,' said Elizabeth. 'Can I go in?'

'Yes,' said Matron. 'You can stay for twenty minutes, till afternoon school. Talk quietly, and don't excite Joan at all.'

Elizabeth went in. She shut the door quietly behind her. Joan was lying in a white bed under a big sunny window, and Mrs Townsend was sitting beside her.

'And is this Elizabeth?' asked Mrs Townsend with a welcoming smile. Elizabeth went forward and shook hands, thinking that Mrs Townsend didn't look very angry after all. She bent over and kissed her friend.

'I'm so glad you're better, Joan,' she said. 'I do miss you.'

'Do you really?' said Joan, pleased. 'I've missed you too.'

'Come here, Elizabeth,' said Mrs Townsend, drawing Elizabeth to her. 'I want to thank you for your letter. I was so surprised to get it – and I know it must have been hard to write.'

'Yes, it was,' said Elizabeth. 'I was awfully afraid you would be angry with me when you got it, Mrs Townsend. I meant to make Joan so happy on her birthday – and I didn't think she'd find out it wasn't you who sent the things! I know it was a silly thing to do, now.'

'Never mind,' said Joan's mother. 'It has made things come right in the end!'

'Have they come right?' asked Elizabeth in surprise, looking from Joan to her mother.

'Very right,' said Mrs Townsend, smiling. 'Joan will tell you all we have said, one day, and you will understand how they went wrong. But now I want to tell you that I am very, very glad Joan has such a kind little friend. I know she will be much happier at Whyteleafe now that she has you. It is so horrid to have no friends at all.'

'Oh, Elizabeth, I *do* so wish you were staying on at Whyteleafe,' sighed Joan, taking her friend's hand. 'Couldn't you possibly, possibly stay?'

'Don't ask me to, Joan,' said Elizabeth. 'You know I've made up my mind to go, and it's feeble to change your mind once you've made it up! I've said I shall go, and if the Meeting says I can, I shall go back with my parents when they come to see me at half-term.'

'Do you think *you* will be able to come and see me at half-term?' asked Joan, turning to her mother.

'Yes, I will,' answered Mrs Townsend. 'I hope by then that you will be up and about, and we will go to the next town, and spend the day there, Joan.'

'Oh, good,' said Joan happily. It was the first time her mother had ever come to take her out at half-term, and the little girl was delighted. 'I shall get better quickly now, so that I shall be ready for you at half-term!'

A bell rang in the school. Elizabeth got up quickly. 'That's my bell,' she said. 'I must go. Goodbye, Mrs Townsend, and thank you for being so nice about my letter. Goodbye, Joan. I'm so glad you're happy. I'll come and see you again if Matron will let me.'

She ran off. Mrs Townsend turned to Joan. 'She's a very nice child,' she said. 'How funny that she should have been so naughty at first – and what a pity she wants to leave! She's just the sort of girl that Whyteleafe School would be proud of.'

Elizabeth thought of Rita as she sat in class that afternoon, doing her painting. 'I told Rita I would go to her as soon as I had an answer to my letter,' she thought. 'Well – I haven't ex*actly* had an answer – and yet I *do* know the answer, because Mrs Townsend came herself and told me!'

She wondered if she should go to Rita after tea. What should she tell her? She didn't know!

She need not have worried herself. Miss Belle and Miss Best had sent for Rita that day, and had told her about Elizabeth, and her queer letter to Joan's mother.

'She spent the money her uncle gave her on buying that big birthday cake for Joan, and other presents and cards,' said Miss Belle. 'That is where the money went, Rita!'

'But why didn't Elizabeth say so?' asked Rita, puzzled.

'Because if she explained that, the school would know Joan's unhappiness at being forgotten by her mother,' said Miss Best. 'If Elizabeth had been longer at Whyteleafe School, she would have gone to you, Rita, or to one of the monitors she trusted, and would have asked their advice – but she has been here such a short time, and is such a headstrong, independent child, that she takes matters into her own hands – and gets into trouble!'

'All the same, she has the makings of a very fine girl in her,' said Miss Belle. 'She is fearless and brave, kind and clever, and although she has been the naughtiest, rudest girl we have ever had, that only lasted for a little while.'

'Yes,' said Rita. 'I liked her almost from the beginning, although she has been very difficult. But she really is the sort of girl we want at Whyteleafe. I'm afraid now, though, that she will go home, for we have promised that she shall, if she wants to.'

'You must send for her and have a talk with her, Rita,' said Miss Best. 'She was supposed to come and tell you when she had an answer to her letter to Mrs Townsend, wasn't she? Well – we know the answer now – and it is not an answer that can be explained fully to a School Meeting. Have a talk with Elizabeth, and then decide what to do. I think you will feel that although Elizabeth did wrong, the kindness that was at the bottom of it more than makes up for the upset she caused !'

'Yes, I think so too,' agreed Rita, who had been very interested in all that Miss Belle and Miss Best had told her. She was glad to know that Elizabeth had spent the pound on somebody else, glad that it was only kindness that had caused such a disturbance ! She went out to look for Elizabeth.

It was after tea. Elizabeth was running to see if Matron would let her sit with Joan again. She bumped into Rita round a corner.

'Good gracious ! What a hurricane you are !' said Rita, her breath bumped out of her. 'You're just the person I want to see. Come to my study.'

Rita had a little room of her own, a study all to herself, because she was Head Girl. She was very proud of it, and had made it as nice as she could. Elizabeth had never been in it before, and she looked round in pleasure.

'What a dear little room !' she said. 'I like the blue carpet – and the blue tablecloth – and the pictures and flowers. Is this your very own room ?'

'Yes,' said Rita. 'William has one too. His is just as nice as mine. He is coming here in a minute. Have a sweet, Elizabeth ?'

Rita took down a tin from her small cupboard and offered it to Elizabeth, who at once took a toffee. Elizabeth wondered what Rita and William were going to say to her. There was a knock at the door, and William strolled in.

'Hallo,' he said, smiling at Elizabeth. 'How's the Bold Bad Girl ?'

Elizabeth laughed. She liked William calling her that, though she had hated the name not so very long ago.

'Elizabeth, William and I know now what you spent that pound on, and why you did it,' said Rita. 'And we want to say that we quite see that you couldn't tell the Meeting.'

'And *we* shan't tell the Meeting either,' said William,

sitting down in Rita's cosy arm-chair.

'But won't you have to?' asked Elizabeth in surprise.

'No,' said William. 'Rita and I are the judges of what can be told the Meeting, and what need not be explained, if we think best. We shall simply say that we have had a satisfactory answer and explanation, and that the matter is now finished.'

'Oh, thank you,' said Elizabeth. 'It wasn't really myself I was thinking of, you know, it was Joan.'

'We know that now,' said Rita. 'You tried to do a right thing in a wrong way, Elizabeth! If you had been at Whyteleafe a little longer, you would have done things differently – but you haven't been here long enough.'

'No, I haven't,' said Elizabeth. 'I do see that I have learnt a lot already, but I haven't learnt enough. I wish I was wise like you and William.'

'Well, why not stay and learn to be?' said William with a laugh. 'You are *just* the sort of girl we want, Elizabeth. You would make a fine monitor, later on.'

'Me! A monitor!' cried Elizabeth, most astonished. 'Oh, I'd never, never be a monitor! Good gracious!'

'It may sound funny to you now, Elizabeth,' said William. 'But in a term or two you would be quite responsible and sensible enough to be made one.'

'I'd simply *love* to be a monitor, and sit in the jury!' said Elizabeth. 'Whatever would Mummy say – and Miss Scott, my old governess, would never, never believe it. She said I was so spoilt I would never do anything worth while!'

'You *are* spoilt!' said Rita, smiling. 'But you would soon get over that. What about staying on, Elizabeth, and seeing what you can do?'

'I'm beginning to feel it would be nice,' said Elizabeth. 'But I can't change my mind. I said I meant to go home at half-term, and I'm going to. It's only feeble people that change their minds, and say first one thing and then another. I'm not going to be like that.'

'I wonder where you got that idea from?' said William. 'I mean, the idea that it's feeble to change your mind once it's made up? That's a wrong idea, you know.'

'Wrong?' said Elizabeth, in surprise.

'Of course,' said William. 'Make up your mind about things, by all means – but *if* something happens to show that you are wrong, then it is *feeble* not to change your mind, Elizabeth. Only the strongest people have the pluck to change their minds, and say so, if they see they have been wrong in their ideas.'

'I didn't think of that,' said Elizabeth, feeling puzzled.

'Well, don't puzzle your head too much about things,' said William, getting up. 'I must go. Think about what we have said, Elizabeth. The next Meeting will be your last one, if you are leaving us – and we shall keep our word to you and let you go if you want to. You can tell your parents when they come to see you at half-term, and Miss Belle and Miss Best will explain everything to them. But we shall be sorry to lose the naughtiest girl in the school!'

Elizabeth left the study, her head in a whirl. She did like William and Rita so much. But she couldn't change her mind – she would be so ashamed to climb down and say she had been wrong.

23 Elizabeth fights with herself

The next day or two were very pleasant. Elizabeth was allowed to see Joan whenever she liked, and she took her some more flowers from John. She also took her a jigsaw puzzle from Helen, and a book from Nora.

Joan was looking very pretty and very happy. Her mother had gone, leaving behind her a big box of velvety peaches, a tin of barley sugar, and some books. But best of all she had left Joan a promise that never, never would she let Joan think she was forgotten again!

'It's all because of *you*, Elizabeth,' said Joan, offering her friend a barley sugar to suck. 'Oh, Elizabeth – do please stay on at Whyteleafe. Don't make me unhappy by leaving, just as I've got to know you!'

'There are plenty of other people for you to make friends with,' said Elizabeth, sucking the barley sugar.

'I don't want them,' said Joan. 'They would seem feeble after you, Elizabeth. I say – have you been looking after my rabbit for me?'

'Of course,' said Elizabeth. 'Oh, Joan, it's the dearest little thing you ever saw! Really it is. Do you know, it knows me now when I go to feed it, and it presses its tiny woffly nose against the wire to welcome me! And yesterday it nuzzled itself into the crook of my arm and stayed there quite still till the school bell rang and I had to go.'

'Harry came to see me this morning and he said he wishes you were not leaving, because he wants to give us two more baby rabbits, to live with my tiny one,' said Joan. 'He said they could be between the two of us.'

'Oh,' said Elizabeth, longing for the two rabbits. 'Really, if I'd known what a nice place Whyteleafe School was, I'd never have made up my mind to leave it!'

She had to go then, because it was time for her music-lesson. She rushed to get her music. Richard was in the music-room, waiting for her with Mr Lewis.

The two were getting on well with their duets. Richard was pleased with Elizabeth now, for he knew that she really loved music, as he did, and was willing to work hard at it. They played two duets very well indeed for Mr Lewis.

'Splendid!' he said. 'Elizabeth, I'm pleased with you. You've practised well since your last lesson, and got that difficult part perfect now. Now – play Richard your sea-piece that you love so much.'

Elizabeth was proud to play to Richard, for she thought him a wonderful player. She played her best. Mr Lewis and Richard listened without a word or a movement till she had finished.

'She ought to play that at the school concert at the end of the term,' said Richard, when the piece was ended. 'It's fine!'

Elizabeth glowed with pleasure. She liked praise from Richard even more than praise from the music-master.

'That's what *I* suggested to her,' said Mr Lewis, sitting down at the piano and playing some beautiful chords. 'But she doesn't want to.'

'I *do* want to!' cried Elizabeth indignantly. 'It's only that I'm leaving soon.'

'Oh – that silly old story again,' said Richard in disgust. 'I thought better of you, Elizabeth. You can stay here if you want to – but you're just too jolly obstinate for words. Your music may be good – but I don't think much of your common sense.'

He stalked off without another word, his music rolled under his arm. Elizabeth felt half angry, half tearful. She hated being spoken to like that by Richard.

'I expect Richard is disappointed with you because I know he hoped that you and he would play the duets in the concert this term,' explained Mr Lewis. 'He'll have to play them with Harry now – and though Harry likes music, he's not a good player.'

Elizabeth finished her music-lesson without saying very much. She was thinking hard. She was in a muddle. She wanted to stay – and she wanted to go, because her pride told her to keep her word to herself and leave.

She went out to do some gardening when her lesson was

over. She and John had become very friendly indeed over the garden. Elizabeth did not mind working hard with John, and he was pleased.

'So many of the others like to pick the flowers, and trim the hedges when they feel like it,' he said, 'but hardly anybody really works *hard*. When the tiny plants have to be bedded out, or the kitchen garden has to be hoed, who is there that offers to do it? Nobody!'

'Well, aren't I somebody?' demanded Elizabeth. 'Don't I come?'

'Oh yes – but what's the use of *you*?' said John. 'You're leaving soon, aren't you? You can't take a real interest in a garden that you won't ever see again. If you were going to stay I would make all my plans with you – I believe Mr Johns would let you take part-charge of the garden with me. It really would be fun.'

'Yes – it would,' said Elizabeth, looking round the garden. 'Are you the head of the garden, John?'

'Yes – under Mr Johns,' said John. 'Nobody needs to garden unless they like, you know – but if it's anyone's hobby, as it is mine, they are allowed to spend most of their spare time here. I've had charge of the garden for two years now, and it's pretty good, don't you think so?'

'Oh yes, I do,' said Elizabeth, looking round it. 'It's lovely. I could think of lovely things for it too, John. Don't you think a row of double pink hollyhocks would be nice, looking over that wall?'

'Fine!' said John, standing up from his hoeing. 'Fine! We could get the seeds now and plant them – and we could set out the new little plants this autumn, ready to flower next summer. Let's ask for money for the seeds at the next Meeting, shall we?'

'Well – you can, if you like,' said Elizabeth. 'I'm afraid it will be my last Meeting, John.'

'Your last Meeting!' said John scornfully, and he dug his hoe into the hard ground as if he were digging it into a Meeting. 'What a feeble goose you are, Elizabeth.'

'Feeble!' cried Elizabeth angrily. 'I like *that*! Just

because I'm keeping my word and sticking to what I said, you call me feeble.'

'Well, it *is* feeble to give up everything you like so much here – your gardening – your riding – your friend – and your music – just because you're too proud to climb down and change your mind,' said John. 'I'm disappointed in you.'

Elizabeth stamped off in a rage. She hated to be called feeble. It was the one thing she had always thought that she wasn't.

She went to the swings. There was no one else there. Elizabeth sat on the highest swing and began to sway to and fro. She thought very hard.

'Now let's get things clear in my own mind,' said Elizabeth to herself. 'First of all – I didn't want to come here, and I vowed to myself, to Mummy and Miss Scott that I'd get sent home as soon as possible. Well, I got the Meeting to say I *could* leave at half-term, and I was jolly pleased. I'd got what I wanted!'

Elizabeth swung high, and the swing creaked as it went to and fro.

'Yes – I'd got what I wanted,' said Elizabeth. 'I needn't even stay a term at this horrid, hateful school. That was what I called it.'

'And now I find it isn't horrid or hateful. I can't help being happy here. The others seem to like me now that I've given up being so awful. I have a friend who is longing for me to stay and will be unhappy when I go. I've disappointed Richard, who wants to play with me at the concert. I've disappointed Mr Lewis. John is angry with me because I don't like his garden enough to stay – though really I do like it awfully. And Harry wants to give me those lovely rabbits.'

She swung even higher as her thoughts sped along.

'And why am I going? Now I'll just be really honest with myself. I'm *not* going because I'm unhappy. I'm very happy now. I'm going simply because I can't bear to change my mind and say I'm wrong. I'm too proud to say

I'll stay, when I've said I'll go. I'm not strong enough to change my mind, and own up I'm wrong!'

Elizabeth slowed down the swing and put her feet on the ground. She frowned and looked at the grass. She had never thought so hard in her life. She spoke to herself sternly.

'Elizabeth Allen, you're feeble! Richard is right and Harry is right. You're feeble! You're a coward! You don't dare to stand up at the next Meeting and say you're too happy to leave! You aren't strong enough to change your mind! You're proud and silly! Elizabeth Allen, I'm ashamed of you!'

Elizabeth spoke these words to herself more sternly than anyone had ever spoken to her. She stopped for a moment, thinking deeply.

'But *am* I really so silly? *Am* I really so feeble? Can I really spoil my happiness here, and Joan's too, by being so stupid and proud? No, I can't! I'm stronger than I thought. I *can* change my mind! I *will* change my mind! What did William say? He said that only the strongest people could change their minds when they saw they were wrong – it was the feeble ones who *couldn't*!'

She began to swing again. 'Well, I'm strong!' she sang, as she swung. 'I can change my mind! I can say I'm wrong! Elizabeth Allen, you're not such a poor thing as I thought! Just wait till the next Meeting – and I'll give them the biggest surprise they've ever had!'

The little girl laughed as she swung. She felt very happy. She was no longer obstinate and proud. She was strong enough to change her mind.

'I wish the next Meeting would come soon!' she said to herself. 'What a shock I shall give them!'

24 A surprise for the school

The last Meeting before half-term met at the same time as usual in the gym. Everyone was there except Joan, who was in the San. rapidly getting better.

Elizabeth sat on her usual form, between Harry and Belinda, feeling rather excited. What a surprise she was going to give everyone!

The ordinary business of the Meeting went through as usual. Money was taken from the box, but none was put in. Most of the children were expecting money from their parents when they saw them at half-term, and the next week the box would be very full again!

A few complaints were made, and one or two reports. Doris, who owned the guinea-pigs, beamed when her monitor reported that she had not forgotten her pets once.

'And,' said the monitor, 'they look the finest guinea-pigs I've ever seen now.'

'Good,' said Rita. 'See that they keep like that, Doris!'

Then Elizabeth's turn came, at the end of the reports. Rita knocked on the table with the mallet, and everyone was silent.

'I haven't much to say about Elizabeth Allen this week,' said Rita. 'But I must just say this – both William and I know now why Elizabeth spent so much money and what she spent it on. We are quite satisfied about it, and we hope that the jury and the rest of you will accept our word when we say that we can only say that we are satisfied, and not tell you any more. Elizabeth was wrong to do what she did, but she was right not to tell us about it. Now the matter has come right, and we have no more to say.'

'Wait, Rita,' said William. 'We *have* more to say! This is the Meeting at which we were to ask Elizabeth if she wanted to leave us – it is our half-term Meeting. Well – we are keeping our word to you, Elizabeth. If you want to go, and you have made up your mind to do so, we give you our permission. Miss Belle and Miss Best will tell your parents, and if they agree, you may go back with them when they see you tomorrow.'

Elizabeth stood up. Her cheeks were flaming red, and her voice was not quite the same as usual.

'I've got something to say,' she said. 'It's not very easy – and I don't quite know how to say it. But anyway, it's this – I'm not going!'

'Not going!' cried everyone in surprise, turning to look at Elizabeth.

'But why not?' asked Rita. 'You said you had made up your mind to go, and that you never changed your mind.'

'Well, William said that only feeble people never change their mind if they know they are wrong,' said Elizabeth. 'And I know I was wrong now. I only made up my mind to be as naughty as possible because I was angry at being sent to school when I didn't want to go, and I vowed I'd go back home as soon as possible, just to show I'd have my own way. Well, I like Whyteleafe. It's a lovely school. And I want to stay. So I've changed my mind, and though you've said I can have what I want, and it's very nice of you, I don't want it now! I want to stay – that is, if you'll let me after all I've done!'

Everyone began to talk at once. Harry thumped Elizabeth on the back. He was very pleased. John nodded at her in delight. Now she could help him with the garden! Richard actually left his place and came to whisper to her.

'You're a good sort,' he said. 'You can play the game as well as you play the piano.'

William banged with the mallet. 'Richard, go back to your place!'

Richard went back, grinning. Belinda and Helen smiled

at Elizabeth, trying to catch her eye. Everyone seemed as pleased as could be.

'Elizabeth!' said William, 'we are very pleased with you. You've made a lot of silly mistakes, but you have made up for them all – and we admire you for being able to change your mind, admit you were wrong, and say so to us all! You are the sort of person we want at this school. We hope you will stay for years, and do your very best.'

'I will,' said Elizabeth, and she meant it. She sat down, looking happy and excited. It was lovely that everyone was pleased. She wasn't the Bold Bad Girl any more – she was Elizabeth Allen, the sort of person that Whyteleafe School wanted. She was proud and happy.

The Meeting ended soon after that – and Elizabeth sped off to the San. to find Joan. Joan was sitting up in a chair, reading.

'Hallo!' she said. 'What happened at the Meeting? Anything exciting?'

'Well – the Meeting said I could go home with my parents tomorrow,' said Elizabeth. 'So I got my own way, you see.'

'Oh, Elizabeth – I *shall* miss you so!' said Joan.

'You won't!' said Elizabeth. 'Because, you see, I'm not going! I'm staying on! I've changed my mind, Joan. I love Whyteleafe, and I won't leave it for years and years and years! Oh, what fun we'll have together! We'll be monitors one day – think of that! Shan't we be grand?'

'Good gracious!' said Joan, so delighted that she hopped out of her chair, and flung her arms round her friend. 'I can't believe it! Oh, I do feel so glad.'

Matron came into the room and looked horrified to see Joan out of her chair.

'What are you doing?' she said sternly. 'I shan't let Elizabeth come in here if that's the way you behave, Joan!'

'But, Matron, I was so pleased because Elizabeth is staying on instead of leaving,' said Joan, sinking back into her chair.

'Dear me! Fancy being pleased because a bad girl like this is staying with us!' said Matron, with a twinkle in her eye.

The girls laughed. They liked Matron – she was cheerful and friendly, though strict. She gave Joan some medicine, and went out.

'We shall have a lovely half-term now,' said Joan. 'My mother's coming to take me out. Is yours coming too?'

'Yes, I had a letter this morning,' said Elizabeth. 'Oh, Joan – let's ask our mothers to take us out together! That would be much more fun than going alone.'

'Yes, we will,' said Joan happily. 'I am sure I shall be well enough tomorrow to get up properly. Now you'll have to go, Elizabeth. That's the supper-bell.'

'Well, I'll see you tomorrow,' said Elizabeth. 'What fun we'll have! Oh, I *am* glad I'm not going home with my mother tomorrow. I wonder what she'll say when she hears that I want to stay on. Every letter I've written to her I've told her that I want to leave!'

Mrs Allen was *very* much astonished when she saw Elizabeth the next day. The little girl looked so bright and happy – her mouth was no longer sulky, and there was no sign of a frown at all! Elizabeth flung herself into her mother's arms and hugged her.

'It's lovely to see you, Mummy,' she said. 'Do come and see everything – the playroom, and my classroom, and our bedroom – it's number 6 – and the garden – and everything!'

Her mother followed Elizabeth round, marvelling at the change in her little girl. *Could* this really be Elizabeth – this good-mannered, polite, happy child? Everyone seemed to like her. She had lots of friends, especially the gentle Joan, who seemed to be Elizabeth's special friend.

'Well, Elizabeth, you're quite a different child!' said her mother at last. 'Oh, look – there is Miss Best. I must just have a word with her.'

'Good morning, Miss Best,' said Mrs Allen. 'Elizabeth

has just been showing me round – and really, she does seem so happy and jolly. What a change you have made in her! I feel quite proud of her!'

'She has made a change in herself,' said Miss Best, smiling her lovely smile. 'You know, Mrs Allen – she was the naughtiest girl in the school – yes, she really was! It was difficult to know what to do with her – but she knew what to do with herself. One of these days she will be the *best* girl in the school, and how proud you will be of her then!'

'Then you want to stay on, Elizabeth?' said her mother in astonishment. 'Well, I *am* glad! What a surprise!'

Mrs Townsend arrived to see Joan at that minute, and Elizabeth ran to see if Joan was ready. She had been kept in bed to breakfast, but was to get up afterwards and allowed to go in her mother's car. She was tremendously excited.

'It's the first time I've ever had a half-term treat like this!' she chattered excitedly, as Elizabeth helped her to dress quickly. 'And it's all because of *you*, Elizabeth!'

'Oh, rubbish!' said Elizabeth. 'Hurry up, Joan. What a time you take with your stockings. We're going to have lunch at a hotel – fancy that! I hope there will be strawberry ice-creams, don't you?'

Joan was ready at last, and the two girls went to find their mothers, who had already made friends. Then they settled down in Mrs Townsend's car, for she said she would drive them all.

'Now we're off for our treat!' said Elizabeth happily, as the car sped through the archway. She looked back at the beautiful building.

'Goodbye for a little while!' she said. 'I'm coming back to you, and I'm glad it's not goodbye for ever!'

We must say goodbye too, though maybe we will see Elizabeth again, and follow her exciting adventures at Whyteleafe School. Goodbye, Elizabeth – naughtiest girl in the school!

ENID BLYTON

If you are an eager Beaver reader, perhaps you ought to try some of our exciting Enid Blyton titles. They are available in bookshops or they can be ordered directly from us. Just complete the form below, enclose the right amount of money and the books will be sent to you at home.

☐	THE CHILDREN OF CHERRY-TREE FARM	£1.99
☐	THE CHILDREN OF WILLOW FARM	£1.99
☐	NAUGHTY AMELIA JANE	£1.50
☐	AMELIA JANE AGAIN	£1.50
☐	THE BIRTHDAY KITTEN ·	£1.50
☐	THE VERY BIG SECRET	£1.50
☐	THE ADVENTUROUS FOUR	£1.50
☐	THE ADVENTUROUS FOUR AGAIN	£1.50
☐	THE NAUGHTIEST GIRL IS A MONITOR	£1.95
☐	THE NAUGHTIEST GIRL IN THE SCHOOL	£1.95
☐	THE ENCHANTED WOOD	£1.99
☐	THE WISHING-CHAIR AGAIN	£1.99
☐	HURRAH FOR THE CIRCUS	£1.75

If you would like to order books, please send this form, and the money due to:
ARROW BOOKS, BOOKSERVICE BY POST, PO BOX 29, DOUGLAS, ISLE OF MAN, BRITISH ISLES. Please enclose a cheque or postal order made out to Arrow Books Ltd for the amount due including 22p per book for postage and packing both for orders within the UK and for overseas orders.

NAME ....

ADDRESS ....

....

Please print clearly.

Whilst every effort is made to keep prices low it is sometimes necessary to increase cover prices at short notice. Arrow Books reserve the right to show new retail prices on covers which may differ from those previously advertised in the text or elsewhere.